THIEVES STALKED SLOCUM!

The man was taken completely by surprise as Slocum's arm snaked around his neck, clinching his throat and shutting off his breath, while at the same time a fist hard as a ramrod slammed into his lower back...

Slocum sat back on his heels. He was listening ...It would have been an easy trap if his quarry had been working with Cooch and Emil and the pair had then bushwhacked him. An old trick; but any trick, old or new was deadly when it worked.

OTHER BOOKS BY JAKE LOGAN

JAKE LOGAN

DEATH TRAP

BERKLEY BOOKS, NEW YORK

DEATH TRAP

A Berkley Book/published by arrangement with
the author

PRINTING HISTORY
Berkley edition/March 1989

ISBN: 0-425-11541-0

A BERKLEY BOOK ® TM 757,375
Berkley Books are published by The Berkley Publishing Group,
200 Madison Avenue, New York, N.Y. 10016.
The name "BERKLEY" and the "B" logo
are trademarks belonging to Berkley Publishing Corporation.

PRINTED IN THE UNITED STATES OF AMERICA

10 9 8 7 6 5 4 3 2 1

1

From the high lip of the coulee John Slocum watched the caravan of horse-drawn Conestogas. There were five wagons pulled by clearly tired teams. Undoubtedly they had come a long way, and he supposed they still had a long way to go. Below, in the immensity of the flat prairie, the train looked small and lonely. He knew now that they were in danger. He had seen the mirror signaling on the tableland up ahead.

Now he had his eyes on the point rider, who was well ahead of the lead wagon. He read the man's movements, realizing his inexperience. And, too, there was the startling fact that they were driving directly into the setting sun, a favorite time for Indian attack.

And at once they came screaming out of a hidden draw, while the final brilliance of the prairie sun was in the eyes of the wagon drivers. Without even a thought, Slocum turned the spotted Appaloosa, unlimbering his Sharps. In a moment they had dropped from view behind a long row of high rocks and now raced down toward the shooting. The pony, which he'd only recently broken himself, handled perfectly. And in moments Slocum was within the range he wanted. He dropped out of the saddle, ground-hitched the horse, and took up a firing position with both his Sharps and his Winchester.

The wagon train had tried to pull into a circle; a tall man on a flea-bitten gray horse with brown and black freckles was screaming orders. But they were late; the Sioux were already circling, firing guns as well as arrows. One of the wagons, caught by a lighted arrow, was aflame. Yet the immigrants were firing back, and Slocum's keen ear realized they had Henrys.

Using the old tactic of changing his position behind the rocks every time he fired, while bellowing orders in different voices and even answering himself, Slocum gave the impression of a multiple attack. The Sioux would of course be wise to such a trick, yet they couldn't be sure. The cleverness of Slocum's positionings, plus the validity of the feared buffalo gun, made them cautious. He also used the trick of reloading after each shot when he alternated with his Winchester, thus avoiding the long pause that would have been necessary if he'd emptied his gun all at once, and the Sioux would have realized he was actually alone.

The Sharps, of course, was deadly, but Slocum also used the Winchester to good advantage. It wasn't long before he heard the eagle bone whistle, and the braves spun their horses and galloped away, taking one dead and one wounded warrior with them, and leaving behind two slightly wounded whites.

The sun was almost at the horizon when he rode out to meet the grateful immigrants. Their wagonmaster was the Reverend Elihu Soames Burlingame, recently resigned pastor of the First Baptist Church in St. Louis.

Along with him were his wife, Charlotte, and their daughter, Sarah, who was holding a kitten in her arms.

The Reverend Burlingame was a tall, grainy-looking man somewhat older than his wife, who, Slocum judged, could hardly be thirty. The reverend was easily a man of fifty, slim yet not without vigor. Slocum noted the determined line of his mouth. He also noticed that his upper lip appeared much lighter than the rest of his face, as though he had recently shaved off a heavy mustache. But he was not used to horses; he sat the flea-bitten gray uncomfortably.

It was more enjoyable to look at his young wife, who had her long brown hair done up on top of her head, and who must have had a certain difficulty in squeezing such vigorous-looking breasts into her calico dress. Slocum was sure he saw her nipples harden as his eyes addressed that part of her firm yet supple body. Indeed she swept her blue eyes swiftly away from him as he looked up at her on the wagon box.

"I would like to invite you to join us, Mr. Slocum," the reverend was saying. "Sir, we do need a man who knows the country; a man who knows how to handle the redskins." The voice was deep, resonant with authority, but Slocum also detected oil. Well, nothing wrong with that, he was thinking. It was surely not easy making a living with a family on your hands and with no sizable flock to offer support.

"We are heading west, as you can see," the reverend went on, as though following a train of thought both he and Slocum were sharing. "We're looking for a place to settle. A town, even a hamlet where we can bring the word of the Lord. And"—he dropped benign eyes to the young girl at his side—"raise our children."

"Thought you might be heading for Oregon," Slocum said. "Most of the wagons are."

"We'll settle for any likely place," Charlotte Burlingame said, speaking for the first time. "I teach school. So I don't think we'll do badly."

"Schools are needed out here," Slocum pointed out, glad that she had finally entered the conversation.

"But will you consider my offer?" the reverend asked.

Slocum reached up and pushed at the brim of his hat, tipping it onto the back of his head. "Don't mind for a spell," he said. "Maybe till we get out of this country anyway."

"What *is* this country?" Charlotte asked. "Is there something special about it?"

"Only for the Sioux," Slocum said. "It's their country, and right now they don't care for visitors."

"I gathered that," the reverend said sourly. "I had already drawn that conclusion." He pursed his pale lips and squinted into the sunset.

"I'll scout you up to the Little Muddy, 'least," Slocum said. "You're already headed in that direction."

"The Little Muddy?" Charlotte Burlingame canted her head toward him in a way that he found delightful. But he was also aware that her husband was watching him.

"The Little Missouri River. There's a one-horse town, I've been told." He touched the brim of his hat in salute to each of them and turned toward the Appaloosa. "I'll do a little scouting ahead, then come in for some grub."

From that time on Slocum kept well to himself, riding point, the flanks, and keeping a sharp eye on their back trail. And so he had little time with either the reverend or his wife, save to nod or say a how-de-do. And no time whatever with the other members of the train.

He had more or less assumed that the immigrants were like any of the wagon train families he had encountered who were westering; and while he did find the reverend rather different from the few men of the cloth he had encountered in the past, he wasn't especially struck by any untoward behavior. The man kept the Good Book always at hand, and more often than not was seen reading it.

Slocum had no trouble at all in putting Elihu Burlingame out of his mind. And he was even glad that he had run into him. The wagon train offered a good cover for him if the party from Medicine Gap who had been so interested in his departure from that town should show up.

A day and a half later they arrived at the Little Muddy.

John Slocum's hair had the blackness of a raven's wing, a perfect accompaniment for his tiger-green eyes. And the muscular yet lithe six-foot-one-inch body stacked under those broad shoulders easily dominated whatever company he was in. This was so even with the occasional taller, bigger man. Some said it was his incredibly supple body, some said it was his eyes; and some claimed it was simply that he was Slocum. Women, it was often said, simply had to take him lying down.

At the moment, however, Slocum wasn't thinking about women as he spent less time than it takes a grown man to shave in giving the town the once-over.

To begin with, he would have been the first to agree that the railroad people had shown less than originality in naming the place. They might as well have used a number, he decided. But history, he reflected right away, is often like that: casual, bowing to inertia.

At the same time, being above all a practical man himself, Slocum had no complaint. The place was good enough for his purpose of the moment, which was as a layover, and preferably out of the way.

Later, and through no particular curiosity on his part, he somehow pieced it together, in the way one gathers, information without especially noticing, and suddenly there is a picture for the memory, and maybe even for the telling.

Evidently the railway crew laying track for the Northern Pacific had picked the site for a section camp. Somebody whose name had escaped even local history, had called it after the river that ran by: Little Missouri.

Someone, holding up the bar when Slocum ordered a beer at the Sure Shot, had observed that sure enough the town was "way the hell and gone from nowhere," or as another observer put it, "forty miles north of hell."

In fact, they were 200 miles north of the newly dis-covered gold fields around Deadbush and—equally in-teresting—180 miles west of the nearest sheriff or U.S. marshal, at Drover. There had been a short-lived mine that had failed, eliminating any possibility of prosperity, as well as dealing a blow to the railroad. And yet, Slo-cum swiftly realized, since the Little Missouri flowed north, the town was fairly accessible to the wilds of Canada; a not small convenience for those who had no burning wish to encounter the law at their heels.

Slocum quickly learned that such personages made up a good piece of Little Missouri's population after the completion of the Northern Pacific. The census, of ne-cessity, had abruptly reduced itself after the construction crew had gone, leaving behind principally those persons who made their living off their fellows—the saloon-keeper, the hotel proprietor, the storekeeper, the livery-man, and last but never least, the gambling-house operator; plus assorted hangers-on, shills, and a covey of "soiled doves."

There were also honest ranchers, trappers, and hunters in the area. These had dubbed the town "Little Misery" and only went there when they needed to. The flooding of the Mud River Mine had doomed any possibility of prosperity.

Little Misery, with its log huts, its unpainted, weather-beaten frame buildings, and its tent houses was now very much a hangout for rustlers, horse thieves, and other unsavory characters who threw a wide loop. Still, there was minimal commerce of a sort.

The town wasn't at all surprised by the arrival of the Reverend Elihu Soames Burlingame and his attractive young wife, nor by the assortment of individuals accompanying them.

Or was it? As it turned out, the day following the wagon train's arrival happened to be Sunday. And to the astonishment of all, the Reverend Burlingame decided to preach a sermon. Since there was no such thing as a church or other house of worship in Little Misery—not even a schoolhouse to hold the service in—the reverend spoke to his gathering outdoors, the members consisting of all the wagon train people plus a handful of local hangers-on. Some of these latter were too inebriated to appreciate the service, while others were too inebriated not to.

All in all, the reverend won the respect of the entire flock.

"Doggone God," he began, his deep, plangent voice

addressing the morning sky. "All along the trail He's given us nothing but dust and misery, and He's by golly going to give us more of the same, but—by God—He's kept us from hunger and He's kept us from getting sick. You and I can eat dust and we can get tired as hell, but we can't stand being sick. Long as He lets us stay well, and gives us enough to eat, He's the greatest God of all, better'n anybody else's! To Him we lift our eyes and our hearts this proud morning in thankfulness. We finally got here in one piece. Hooray for God!"

At which point the town rang with wild cheers.

Slocum noted that during the service a number of others had been drawn to the reverend's noble words. He looked over at Charlotte Burlingame, who was leading the group in song, and saw that she was looking at him. Instantly she dropped her eyes and at the same time missed a note.

Slocum felt good about that.

He felt good about it, while noticing that the reverend kept a tight eye on his mate. At the same time, he knew that Charlotte, so young, so lithe, and, he was sure, so potentially full of life, was drawn to him. Still, he didn't need that kind of trouble. On the other hand, of course, you didn't have to turn someone in need away from your door.

In any event, it was more than clear that the arrival of the wagon train had brought something to Little Misery; and it wasn't just numbers, customers for the saloon, the hotel, or the local eatery. For actually, now that the members of the train had left their wagons outside town and were inhabiting the single street and its few places of congregation, such as the saloons and the general store, the hotel and the eatery, Slocum began to see them in a fresh light.

For instance, there were three young men in their early twenties whom he wouldn't exactly have pegged as choirboys. One looked like an out-and-out tough, another had a sneer that seemed never to leave his face, while the third carried a swagger that also spelled trouble. And there was a suspicious bulge in more than one coat. On the afternoon of their arrival in town he came upon the three playing pretty sharp poker in the Sure Shot. And finally, a couple of the younger women seemed not only unattached but highly attachable, judging from the way they eyed one or two of the male inhabitants of Little Misery. In short, Slocum began to wonder just what sort of wagon train he'd been guiding those past two days and a night. If they were immigrants "westering," as the Reverend Burlingame had put it, they were not like any immigrants he'd ever seen— not outside a saloon or gambling house.

He had decided now to watch Burlingame more closely, for the man was a surprise, maybe even more so than the people in his care. For it was clear that underneath the reverend's down-home religion ran a vein of steel. Something in his eyes, yes. But more: in his whole manner, really.

However, it was the morning after their arrival in the strange little town that the question of the reverend and his wagon train, which had begun to intrigue him, was all at once swept into the background. And his surprise was shared by the denizens of Little Misery and the members of the wagon train both. And in the most astonishing manner.

2

The conveyance, as a local worthy called it, had evidently arrived in the dead of night. The like of it had never before appeared in Little Misery. That first morning a number of the townspeople must have thought the wages of acute alcoholism had finally reached them.

The conveyance was an extra-long railway coach, elaborately equipped and lavishly decked out with fresh paint and polished brass. In the morning sun it shone like something from a circus or fairyland. It stood on a siding, where it had been shunted some hours earlier by the St. Paul-to-Portland express. Its window shades were drawn, and as the awestruck citizens of Little Misery contemplated it, it showed no sign of life. It was simply there.

"It ain't no caboose," said Clem Abernathy, the proprietor of Little Misery's Hotel de Paris.

"And it for sure ain't no cattle car," said Bill Forefinger, who ran the town livery.

Their companions, named McFadden, Pone, and

O'Gatty, sniffed, spat, scratched themselves, nodded, and spat again in agreement.

Another man now joined them, Three-Card Monte Kitchen, the town's principal gambler-in-residence. Three-Card was wearing the accepted costume of his profession—a dirty, crusty black frock coat, a black string tie, a shirt which at one time must have been white, and a remarkable stovepipe hat.

"Fer Chrissake, don't you assholes know a private railroad car when you see one?"

"Private? You mean—a private coach?"

"I mean money, you idiots. That there cost plenty of dinero, I assure you." Three-Card Monte, who had worked riverboats in his time, liked to regard himself as a man of education. He favored the word "assure" as one that might throw a little awe amongst his companions. At the same time he was thinking how if he played his cards right the visitation of the obviously affluent passengers within the gorgeous railway car could do no harm. And he said so to his fellows, pointing out with no subtlety whatsoever that as a man of the world, which they definitely were not, he would take the lead in the present circumstances.

His companions, having played cards and shot dice and drunk often enough with Monte Kitchen, knew what this meant and were immediately on guard.

"Money!" Three-Card said it as though tasting it, while at the same time turning it over in his mind, letting the potent word fall onto his five companions while they stood there in the morning light, savoring the present spectacle of the railway car, and the future anticipation of "a good bit more than squeezin's, by God!" as Three-Card put it.

Presently, a gray-haired, portly gentleman of astounding dignity—revealed mostly in his starched back and a vast chest, which, under a sharply waxed mustache and grave jowls, seemed to be impatiently expecting medals—appeared on the platform at one end of the car. He regarded the scene past the end of his long, pointed nose. He was wearing a monkey jacket of red velvet, black trousers with silver stripes down the sides, a boiled shirt with a wing collar, and an incredibly white bow tie.

Nor did this person seem at all impressed by the broad stretches of prairie and towering buttes in the distance, and even less moved by what appeared in the foreground: the muddy Little Missouri, spanned by the Northern Pacific trestle; not to mention the unwashed gaping creatures who formed a semicircle before the awesome conveyance.

Three-Card Kitchen now stepped briskly forward, removed his plug hat, and bowed. "Your Honor, sir, we citizens of—"

"Stop, sir!" The gray-haired man held up both his hands. "I am only a commoner, sir, just as yourself. My name is Pierre, and I am personal valet and secretary to Lord Frederick Edgerton. Lord Frederick and Lady Millecent are within. They have most graciously decided to pay your, uh, community a visit." He paused, and the wings of his large nose flared in a careful sniff. "I want to add that Lord Frederick may spend a certain amount of time here in your quaint village, and wishes to engage in some bison hunting."

"Hell, Frenchy, there ain't no—" Bill Forefinger started to say, when without the slightest warning Three-Card ploughed him one in the rib cage with his elbow.

"There is plenty of buffs around here, you can tell His Lordship," said Three-Card, raising his voice to cover the gaffe that his companion had almost made. "Lotsa bison, buffalo, antelope, deer, elk, the whole kit and caboodle. We'll, uh, find you a good guide, a real good guide."

"That's very good of you," Pierre replied with a cold smile, still sniffing the rank, unwashed odor coming from the sextet.

"Mebbe we could go in an' say how-de-do with His Lordship," put in Clem Abernathy, thinking how he might be able to rent some rooms to the English nobleman and his group.

"Good idea," agreed Packy O'Gatty, the saloon owner of the Sure Shot, dreaming of a brisk business in the immediate future. Hell, he was thinking, maybe there were other men working for this English dude, whoever the hell he was.

Once again Pierre held up his two hands with their chubby palms facing the little group of natives. "A moment! It is customary to, uh, present one's best appearance when meeting Lord Frederick. I suggest you prepare yourselves well before, let us say, this afternoon. Late afternoon," he added, and his eyes moved pointedly up and down the disheveled figures before him.

"Shit take it," said Cy Pone, nudging Elbows McFadden in the side, but gently, and more in humor than anything else. "Thought sure that dude would wanta meet up with us like right now. Didn't you, Elbows?"

"That I did," Elbows agreed, and hiccupped vigorously.

"Gentlemen, let us say four o'clock." Pierre bowed, and then, adding a little nod of his very round head, and touching his waxed mustache at both ends with the thumb and little finger of one hand, he withdrew inside the coach.

The sun was well into the sky now, and its light sprayed the railway coach with fantastic colors. Watching it from the other side of the tracks, Slocum marveled at the way the light changed. He had managed to see the whole scene that had taken place, while remaining out of view to the participants, though this had not been by design but by accident, for he had gone down to the river for an early-morning swim. Yet he had heard almost the whole of the conversation. What he didn't hear, however, was what followed when the gaggle of six withdrew to the Sure Shot for liquid support.

It was said of Little Misery that when you stepped outside any building you were out of town. Another interesting feature of the place was that the population never varied appreciably. No one ever came there, except persons interested in getting lost for a certain while, men with changeable names, gamblers past their prime, or possibly those needing a rest from the attentions of the law or from adversaries with grudges to vent. There were gunmen of varying degrees of ability, but they rarely shot at each other. There was a not unfriendly rivalry between Packy O'Gatty's Sure Shot Drinking and Dancing Establishment and the new tent saloon which went by the name of the Stud. This was run by a giant named The Allen. Nobody knew whether "The" was Mr. Allen's real name or a shortening of Theodore, and nobody particularly wanted to ask.

The Allen was relatively new to Little Misery. He had arrived one evening on a near-foundered horse and had remained. In a town where nobody asked questions, it didn't take long for The Allen to be accepted. In his particular case, it took only a few hours, following the beating he administered to a pretty tough hide skinner resulting from an altercation at the gaming table in the Sure Shot. The skinner had made the mistake of claiming The Allen had been switching tops and flats on him, whereupon he ended up with a broken jaw, a broken nose, and a broken gun hand—after having committed the folly of trying to draw a belly gun on The.

Packy O'Gatty, a man who relied more on his Peacemaker than his fists, ordered Mr. Allen from the Sure Shot premises, though somehow without incurring his enmity. Forthwith, The opened his own drinking establishment. Yet he maintained a satisfactory relationship with Mr. O'Gatty's Sure Shot.

The Stud was at the opposite end of town from the Sure Shot, and it was there that Slocum found himself later on the morning of the arrival of the conveyance bearing the English lord and lady.

The day was hot, and he had decided a beer would be pleasant while he thought out what he would try next. He had brought the wagon train safely to Little Misery and had left them, telling the Reverend Burlingame that now they were on their own. At the same time he advised him to hire a good scout.

"But we would like to have you," Burlingame had said. "How about it?"

Slocum had declined, though somewhat reluctantly as he regarded the buttocks of Charlotte Burlingame, who was just then crossing the street wearing an extremely tight riding skirt. At the same time there was definitely something about the reverend's wagon train that made him cautious—and curious. He knew he couldn't put his finger on it, but there was something there. And so he would wait. He could always change his mind.

The Stud was a short-bit house—10 cents for a drink—instead of a two-bit house such as the Sure Shot where the drinks were 25 cents. The bar was a plank supported by beer kegs, and the standard drink was un-laughingly referred to as snake juice.

Slocum had just settled himself at the bar when in walked the Reverend Elihu Burlingame.

"I've been looking for you, Slocum! So glad I found you!"

"I hope you're not thinking of asking me again to lead your wagon train, Reverend, because my answer is still no."

Burlingame smiled at that, as though he'd been ready for it. "Can I buy you a drink, sir?" he suddenly asked.

"Still got this beer," Slocum said, wondering what the man was up to.

"Mind if I join you, then?"

"It's a free country, I have been told."

"Good, then. I'll be back directly, and maybe we can sit over there." He nodded toward an upturned crate which evidently served as a table, with a broken chair and a second smaller upturned crate next to it, and Slocum picked up his mug of beer and walked over to wait.

He let his glance run over the clientele while he sat there. They were not numerous. The usual crowd, he supposed: a couple of buff runners, or maybe they were wolfers—the smell was more or less the same; and a few cowpunchers, he supposed from nearby cow outfits.

He watched the reverend throw down a shot of whiskey at the bar and then carry a bottle over to where he was sitting.

"Got the ague. Nothing helps it better'n the whiskey," he said confidingly, lowering his big frame onto the chair with the broken back, while enveloping Slocum in his heavy whiskey breath.

"Are you thinking of maybe stopping here?" Slocum asked, just to keep the moment at a friendly level. He was observing Burlingame closely—the man's hard, staring eyes, narrowly spaced, his tight jaw, and his long fingers. He would have bet that those hands were not at all unfamiliar with cards.

"Charlie and myself—I call Charlotte 'Charlie'— talked it over last night. Thought we'd stay around for a spell. Of course, maybe some of the others might want to push on. But there's no church here, no school. There is a need." He leaned forward, and now his voice was lower as he took a quick glance around the room, apparently to make sure no eager listener was within range.

"You have seen the railway car, I am sure," he said.

"Sure have. Looks pretty fancy."

"Have you been inside?"

"Nope. You inviting me?"

A humorless chuckle fell from the reverend's thin lips. "I have."

"Been inside?"

He nodded, lowering both eyelids gently and pursing his lips to emphasize the importance and, evidently, secrecy of the event.

"That why you wanted to talk to me?" Slocum asked, and his voice was firmer now, his words stripped to the essential. He was beginning to wonder more about the reverend's true background.

"Lord Frederick sent for me. A religious question, and I shall not go into it," he said, sniffing wetly.

Whipping out a red bandanna from his back pocket, he wiped vigorously. "Well, uh, he did mention that the town needed a church."

Slocum saw that he was a man who used a lot more strength for a small movement than was necessary. The reverend had whipped out his bandanna the way he would have drawn a gun.

"Let me get to the point, Slocum. Following our conversation, Lord Frederick and I, over a glass of, I must say, excellent sherry, he asked me if I happened to know of a big-game hunter, preferably for buffalo. What he wanted, to be precise, was a guide and I expect companion for his shooting party. The reason for his visit to the Little Missouri country."

"And you suggested me, I take it."

"I did. I did suggest you. But of course, that is up to you. I would wager that the fee would be an agreeable one. I'd like to go along myself, for a matter of fact. Not that I believe in killing God's creatures. I do not! Most emphatically! But for the adventure, the beauty of the wild West in its still primitive state! Ah, it is that experience that draws me. Indeed"—and he held up his right index finger, as though calling for lightning to strike were he not speaking the truth—"indeed, it is the true Call of the Wild that has brought me here. To the Little Missouri country, the West. Yes, brought me to this very day!"

Slocum was almost taken aback at the power of the other man's delivery. His eyes were suddenly wild, gleaming like polished marbles. He shook his head, and Slocum took note of the large lobes that hung from his ears, which were flat as saucers.

Now he shoved his long thin fingers under his wide yellow galluses and scratched his hard belly, as a soft whistle came through his pursed lips. His eyes narrowed. "I recommended you to Lord Frederick, Slocum. I gave you a one-hundred-percent recommendation!"

"I do 'preciate it," Slocum said dryly.

"Sir, I would do the same at the gate of Saint Peter, let me assure you." And leaning forward he slapped the table top with the palm of his hand. A wide grin took over his entire face. "Slocum, I've a voice in me. I know you are a man in trouble. And you could use help in these parlous times. Let me advise you to take on this assignment. You will be helping both Lord Frederick and yourself. And, uh"—his voice dropped to a sly note—"not to mention Lady Millecent."

"A beauty is what you're saying," said Slocum, deciding to go along with the game. There was obviously something more than hunting buffalo, he figured, with the reverend putting out all this bait.

"A, uh, shall we say, a lady of high, the highest quality, and at the same time possessing the true instincts of her gender, plus the necessary physical requirements to satisfy the same." And his loaded eyes lay right into Slocum.

"Might look into it, since you make it sound so . . . sensible."

"It doesn't hurt to look into things. You can always say no."

Slocum grinned. "You make it sound like a man wouldn't want to."

"I am of course speaking only of a man of your caliber, Slocum. May I buy you another beer, sir?"

And suddenly Slocum was again filled with the suspicion he had until then only been vaguely aware of regarding Burlingame. Something? Yes, in that simple

matter of offering to buy him a drink. Funny, that. A
simple enough gesture, and one that would easily have
passed unnoticed. But from what he had noticed so far,
it added up to the reverend being just awfully damn
eager for him to take the job—whatever it turned out to
be—with Lord Frederick Edgerton.

"I'll just settle with one beer for now," Slocum said,
standing up. He stood looking down at the Reverend
Elihu Burlingame, thinking how he would in fact look
into the proposition. Again it might be a good way for
him to drop from sight for a while.

"See you," he said, and started toward the front of
the tent saloon.

Suddenly his attention was caught by a commotion
near the plank bar, where a huge man was shouting a
stream of invective into the face of a young woman.

"You fucking little whore, you been cheating me on
your percentage! Don't tell me you ain't been doin' it!"

"It's not true, The! You're lying!" She spoke quietly,
without raising her voice, yet all heard her in the now
silent tent.

The man was stopped for only an instant, and Slocum looked at the big head, the huge hands, the fierce,
ugly face and, even more dramatic, the menacing
stance. So this was the man he'd heard about, the proprietor of the Stud saloon—The Allen.

"You callin' me a liar!"

"I said you were lying."

In the silence that came from the stalled gathering the
words fell with all the promise of irrevocable disaster.

Slocum had by now moved so that he had a better
view of the participants in the wild drama. To his astonishment, he saw that the girl was a gorgeous creature
who appeared quite foreign to her surroundings. Her

soft blond hair was swept back from her high forehead,
her eyes were sparkling with excitement; she was certainly not terrified, though obviously afraid, as anyone
would be under such circumstances. Her figure did
everything to make the rather plain gown she was wearing absolutely seductive. She was everything the man
was not. The man was a brute. And it wasn't just in his
hideous face, it was in his gnarled, overwhelmingly
powerful body.

Something in Slocum impelled him to move in
closer. There was quite a crowd in the tent now; other
men had entered since the beginning of the confronta-
tion. A large area had expanded around the two participants.

"Nellie, got to say you got balls!" shouted an old-
timer deep in his snake juice from the end of the bar.

A roar went up.

"Think you could say that about The Allen?" she
called out. And a silence fell as though the entire tentful
of people had been poleaxed.

By God, thought Slocum, the girl had her guts for
sure.

"You'll eat those words, you fucking little bitch!"
And the big man, who resembled a buffalo more than
any other animal, reached out a huge paw and grabbed
the girl by the hair.

"Leave it!"

The words snapped out of the tall man with the tiger-
green eyes and raven-black hair. The man with the
broad shoulders, the catlike walk, and the gun holstered
for cross-draw.

"Stay out of it, mister," some voice nearby cau-
tioned. "That's The Allen. Nobody goes up agin him."

In the silence that followed this advice, Slocum

could hear someone sucking his teeth. But he knew it wasn't the reverend who had warned him. Burlingame in fact had moved to the back of the tent, as far away from the scene as he could get.

Meanwhile, The Allen had turned to look at the man who had told him to leave it.

"Make me," he said softly. And without even a glance at the girl he slammed her across the mouth with the back of his hand.

The girl staggered and dropped to her knees, covering her face. And The Allen and John Slocum stood facing each other.

Suddenly The Allen charged, swinging a long, looping overhand right, which, if it had connected, would likely have knocked Slocum through the wall of the tent. But Slocum slipped the punch, bobbed, weaved, and drove a smashing left into his opponent's belly. It felt like he had hit a brick wall.

The next thing he knew The Allen had him in a bear hug, squeezing out his breath, and now back-heeled him. They crashed to the hard ground; the huge man on top of Slocum, now rubbing his stubbled chin into his adversary's eyes.

All at once, Slocum freed one leg and brought his knee up into The Allen's crotch. It was a strong blow, enough to make the giant loosen his grip. Slocum pushed fingers into his huge opponent's eyes, and when The loosened his grip further, chopped the side of his fist into his Adam's apple.

Then he was free and up on his feet. The Allen also rose quickly, and now they circled each other, throwing an occasional punch while the crowd egged them on.

By now the tent must have held almost the entire male population of Little Misery as word got out that

some stranger was taking on the awesome The and was
giving as good as he was getting.

"Come on and fight, you sonofabitch!" the saloon-
keeper roared, spitting blood, and weaving his great
arms and fists in front of him like a pugilist. "Want
Nellie to help you?"

But Slocum wasn't going to spend his breath on talk.
In a flash he saw his opening; he feinted and drove a
short hook right under the other man's ear, with every
ounce of himself behind the blow, bringing it right up
from his feet, his legs, up through his back, his whole
body. The Allen fell like a log to the dirt floor of the
tent.

He lay flat on his belly, his arms outstretched, his
face dug into the dirt that had been churned up by the
battle.

Slocum felt himself starting to heave and was sure he
was going to be sick. The man had been a grizzly. Yet
he had beaten him, and a roar went up from the crowd.
But he wasn't sick. Still out of breath, he straightened
up, tucked his torn shirt back into his trousers, and accepted the glass of beer that the Reverend Burlingame
offered him.

"You got an interesting way of making a feller take
that second beer you offered," Slocum said, still sucking air.

"Mister, you're in big trouble. I don't know if you
know that."

The girl was looking at Slocum earnestly as she sat
across the table from him. They were in the room that
passed for a restaurant on the ground floor of the Hotel
de Paris.

Slocum picked up his cup of coffee and took a long

drink. "Coffee tastes like boiled snake heads," he said. "About like the whiskey I reckon The Allen's selling at the Stud."

The girl nodded. "That's not far off." She leaned forward, her gray eyes looking right at the bridge of his nose. "Listen, The is a tough, cruel, dangerous man. Yes, yes, I know, you beat him, and that was great, but—"

"Nobody's claiming anything's great," Slocum said. "I'm listening. You want me to watch out and be careful. And I do appreciate your concern."

"But you're not going to do anything about it, are you?"

He was looking at her mouth. It was wide, soft, with the lips full and inviting.

When he said nothing, she said, "He isn't that easily beaten. He'll get you next time. Never mind that you won this one, he'll get you—somehow, some way. And he'll get you good. I haven't known him long, but I know his type."

"So . . ." He was leaning on the table, and he shrugged, opening his hands. "So you can't live forever. What do you want me to do—leave town?"

"Next time he'll come at you with a gun—I mean from the back."

"I'm looking forward to it," he said. His eyes had returned to her lips.

"You're not listening to a thing I've been saying."

"That's the first time you've been right."

"I give up."

"I've got a question."

She made a face at him. "I know. I know what it is. You want to know what such a nice girl like me is doing in such a rotten dump."

"You've read my mind. As a matter of fact I was wondering that—word for word."

"Some of us, who aren't romantic cowboys and horsemen riding off into the blazing sunset, have to earn a living."

"A girl—" he started to say, but she cut in.

"A girl like you—so good-looking, and so smart, why are you making a living on your back?"

"Maybe it's you I should've beaten up on," he said, "Or maybe you should just have your ass paddled."

"You like it fancy, huh?"

"I wasn't talking about fancy tricks. I meant it as I said it. You're a smart-aleck."

"Aren't you going to ask me what I charge for it?" she said suddenly.

"I don't pay for it, lady." But though he had meant to say it in a hard way, he somehow didn't.

"I don't do it for pay."

He must have shown his surprise, for she laughed. "Sorry to shock you."

"Then what are you doing in a place like the Stud?"

"I don't put out, Mr. Slocum, but I hire the girls who do."

"I see. Are times that hard?"

"Nothing hard about anything. It's my business."

"Tell me more," he said. "How did you get attracted toward this kind of career, Miss . . ." He had taken the role of someone interrogating her, and she smiled down at her hands.

"O'Leary. But you can call me Nellie."

"Why don't we cut the nonsense and go up to my room," he said, moving as though to get up. He really wanted to see how far she'd go with the game.

"Sorry. I told you I don't put out."

"I thought you just meant professionally."

"Any way."

"You mean—never!"

"Only with the right feeling. I guess I could say it like that."

"So let me know when you get the right feeling, will you? I might still be interested." He leaned back now in his chair. "Do you want another coffee?"

"No thank you."

He stood up. "See you," he said.

"See you."

Slocum stood by the table looking down at her as she remained seated. "I like you, lady."

She looked up at him. "I told you, you could call me Nellie."

He nodded and turned on his heel and started away.

There had been nobody else in the dining room while they were there, and he was just as glad. He was not a man who liked having other people in on his private business.

For a moment he thought of taking a walk, but then he decided to go up to his room. He had only been there maybe five minutes when there came a knock at the door.

"I suddenly remembered that I'd forgotten to tell you something," she said when he opened the door.

"What was that?" he asked, standing back so she could enter.

"I like you too."

"Well, that makes two good things," he said after he had locked the door.

"Two?"

"One—that you're here. And the other—that I was right in expecting you."

She grinned up at him as he slipped his arms around her. "Golly, for once I don't have anything to say."

Slocum didn't have anything to say either. He was busy helping her undress.

3

She was already straddling his erect organ as he pulled off his last article of clothing. Neither of them noted what that was—or cared. The tip of his member was between her wet lips, and now, adjusting herself, she rode down on him while he entered, and they both sank onto the bed, their bodies already undulating in slow tempo, each finding its own way to dance with the other. He was all the way in her, right up to the hilt, and her breath came in spasms as their rhythm increased.

Meanwhile, she was running her hands over his back, down his sides, on his pumping buttocks. He had his left hand under her head, and his right on her left breast, as he bent his lips to her large, pink—and wholly eager—nipple.

"Oh God," she whispered. "Oh God, chew it, suck it, bite it. Use your tongue, your teeth!"

And now, madly, they began to pump together at a quicker tempo, but always in unison, faster and faster and faster—until each exploded at the exact moment together, and as they squirted their come, mixing it in rushes of ecstasy, he drove his cock deeper and she spread herself wider as they rushed to the ultimate.

They lay together, tired, enjoying wholly their joy. Then they slept. And when they awakened each felt a new freshness.

Soon he began to look at her body as he leaned above her, supporting himself on one elbow.

"You like what you see?"

"I sure do. Especially these," he said, touching her firm, flushed breasts.

"And what about . . . ?" Her eyes moved downward.

"And especially this," he said, fondling her bush and wet slit.

"God, you're good," she said.

"It takes two to make it good."

"Thank God for that. It sure beats doing it by yourself."

"Don't you get a lot of men?" he asked.

"I told you, I'm not in the business."

"And I heard you, but you're damned good-looking, and you do it real nice."

"Thank you. I'll always remember that compliment. And I mean it, Slocum." She reached up and pulled him down to her. "I like you. I told you I liked you. Do you understand what I'm saying." Then she said, "I'm sorry. Please forgive me."

He felt her tears on his shoulder.

"Tears are good for you," he said. "So there's no need to be sorry. Only dead people don't cry."

"Thank you."

They had been lying still, and now she reached down and took hold of his rapidly stiffening tool. Bending, she licked its head with her tongue, then slid it into her mouth.

Slocum thought he would come right then, but she backed off, letting him out, coughing.

"God, what a big thing!"

"You make it that way."

"And you make me wet enough to float," she said.

He bent down now and kissed her bush.

"Oh God, Slocum, let's do it a lot. A whole helluva lot!"

"I wasn't planning on going anywhere," Slocum said. And he was up on his hands and knees, while she drew up her legs and spread them so that he could come down on top of her and into her—all the way, with his organ stroking and her loins bucking in exquisite rhythm—all the way to the apex of their great pleasure.

Then they slept. Then they did it again. And again. After a while they lost count.

In order to form the "representative committee of citizens" suggested by Pierre, Lord Frederick's factotum, Three-Card Kitchen and the boys got themselves washed and slicked from head to toe. They had truly caught Three-Card's drift as he outlined the possibilities of separating such a tenderfoot with "nary a corn and nary a callus" from a sizable portion of his wealth. They hadn't slicked themselves up like this in years.

They found Lord Frederick and Lady Millecent awaiting them in the parlor of the private car. Lady Millecent wore a simple and becoming split-skirt riding habit—all beige, with an orange scarf around her neck. The boys were thunderstruck at their first look, for she was everything she was supposed to be, even in their wildest dreams. To begin with, she was beautiful. Her red hair set off her very white face and bright hazel eyes under dark eyebrows. She had a full mouth with full lips, and a delightful beauty spot on her left cheek. Her figure was exquisite. She looked as though she had been poured into her riding habit. When she spoke, she spoke slowly with a very English accent.

Lord Frederick, on the other hand, presented an astounding appearance. He had got himself up in a costume that resembled nothing more than one of the lurid lithographed covers of an eastern Wild West magazine. He was a handsome man with a neat mustache, and he had an athletic build. On the very top of his head he wore an enormous Stetson hat that was too small for him, yet the brim was wider than his broad shoulders. When he moved, it flopped. His chaps were equally huge. As one of the visitors remarked later when the group had retired to the Sure Shot, "I'll betcha that Lord Frederick has to take two steps 'fore one of his chaps can even begin to move."

The Englishman also wore hand-tooled morocco-leather boots that must have cost a minor fortune, while around his slender waist were two ornate cartridge belts with holsters in which reposed a brace of enormous pearl-handled six-guns chased in silver.

This extraordinary figure appeared to be absolutely at home in his costume as he passed around brandy and cigars. Then he opened the meeting, with the supreme assumption that the six self-styled representatives of Little Missouri would be totally willing to help him with his enterprise.

The project he described was unusual, to say the least. With the most adamant sobriety he told the assemblage that he planned to capture whole herds of buffalo and ship them to Chicago alive, for the eastern meat market.

"I know it will work," he explained, reaching for his

brandy. "I might inform you gentlemen that my uncle and my cousin hunted buffalo out here in the Badlands some years ago. And my cousin Edward told me all about it. He told me there were hundreds of thousands of the animals at large, and free for the taking. He said Uncle Harry shot hundreds of them, thousands. I've been told by experts that, while their meat might be considered grainy, nevertheless if prepared well it could be succulent." And in emphasis of this gastronomic prize he kissed the tips of his own fingers. And then he took a good pull on his brandy.

"I of course realize," he continued in his clipped British voice, with all the pomposity of Empire, "I realize that a great deal will have to be done before the enterprise can be got under way. Huge pens in which to hold the buffalo whilst they await shipment must be built close to the railroad. And then we shall require herders to roam the plains and drive the beasts into the pens. Possibly a few dozen such herders will suffice. Now then . . ." Pause. "Now then . . ." He paused once more, deciding on a stiff pull on his brandy, while his company gratefully followed suit. At last he got going again.

"Now then, I, of course, know nothing of the reliability or, on the other hand, the unreliability of the residents hereabouts. As a consequence, in the important matter of hiring a suitable crew, I shall have to put myself wholly in your hands."

By now much of the color had drained from the faces of the six residents of Little Misery. And indeed, Packy O'Gatty, perhaps even more appalled than his companions, almost burst out with a remonstrance that might have spoiled the day. But Three-Card Monte Kitchen stomped on his foot and shut him up in the nick of time.

What O'Gatty had started to say was that buffalo in their native element were as wild and skittish as mountain lions, that nobody had ever succeeded in herding them in quantity, and that even if they could be herded they possessed the weight and strength to break loose from any pen that man could possibly devise.

But this truth remained unspoken, while Three-Card and his companions nodded in eager agreement to Lord Frederick's proposal.

At this point Three-Card capped the triumph over the tenderfoot by declaring, "For sure that is a great idee, Lord! Only one thing, though, and that is that real good buff herders—experienced and all that—they come high, and there ain't but a few in these here parts. Now, what can we—what can *you*—offer to attract them?" And his already heavily lined brow disappeared in a web of wrinkles up toward his receding hairline.

Lord Frederick reached for his cigar, which he had placed carefully in a silver ashtray. Slowly he took a drag and emitted a plume of smoke. His company waited.

"That will, of course, be no problem," he said. "Money is no object. We shall spend as necessary." He rose suddenly and stood before them. "So—good. Get the herders, and meanwhile I shall be fashioning our plan. We shall be in close touch, gentlemen. But first, I want to shoot some buffalo. I have hired a top guide. And we'll talk on my return."

With word and gesture the Englishman had brought them to their feet, and at the same time Pierre arrived to herd them to the door, while Lady Millecent, beautifully silent throughout the exchange, now smiled farewell.

The next thing they knew they were outside the conveyance looking back at the closed carriage door.

"Jesus," someone said softly.

"Holy Shit!" Three-Card Kitchen whipped off his plug hat and instantly returned it to his head. "Holy shit!" he repeated.

In solemn silence, and without anyone suggesting it, the six walked to the more familiar ground of the Sure Shot, there to recap the event and to develop their own plan to increase their dwindling funds.

More than one person had made the statement that The Allen was surely the ugliest man alive. The Reverend Elihu Soames Burlingame now made the very same observation—to himself—but with the slight rephrasing that The was surely the ugliest man "ever born of woman." Even though Elihu Burlingame was no legitimate member of the clergy, he had all his adult life thrown a religious cast on observations that came within his scrutiny.

The two men were alone in the tent house behind the Stud, which The Allen was using for his home. The's bedroll was in one corner, and in the center of the dwelling was a wood stove, not lighted, which took up a lot of space. There were three chairs, an upended crate in case a fourth seat was needed, a table, and a small kitchen range, though The never cooked. He ate his meals at the Doggone Eatery, at the other end of town.

At the moment, The and the reverend were enjoying a drink of whiskey. They had fallen silent, having already covered Elihu's meeting up with Slocum, and how Lord Frederick, on Elihu's recommendation had engaged him as a scout.

"I found it a disappointment that you allowed Slocum to whip you, Allen," Burlingame said suddenly, following out the line of thought that had been running through him.

The Allen ran his big palm along the side of his neck. "Let him feel the confident; I'll kill the sonofabitch next time," he said, his voice rattling like a box of loose gravel. "That bugger don't fight fair." He spat suddenly and viciously in the direction of the jumbo stove, hitting it on its side. He sniffed, ran his hand over his hideous face, and—so the reverend assumed—smiled.

It was said that The had been in a gas explosion when a young boy. One side of his face was definitely lower than the other. His right eye could hardly be seen by anyone looking directly at him, though The could see out of it. His nose had obviously been broken more than once, while both ears had been pummeled in so many fistfights that they were thoroughly cauliflowered.

"I'll even it with the sonofabitch when I'm ready," The promised. "This way, he'll be spreading himself, singing a brag, and be more likely to take our handling, is how I sees it."

"There is some sense in that," the reverend agreed. He was surprised at The's losing the fight with Slocum. A lucky punch? But maybe it was all right. The man might be easier to use, flushed with all that good feeling about himself. And then, The Allen, though he'd once fought professionally as a bareknuckler, was past his prime. He was still powerful, but no longer the man who had fought John C. Heenan and Paddy Ryan. The point was, as he had pointed out to The, the point was to use Slocum, and that clearly was not going to be easy. But now he might be overconfident, and thus not so sharp. It was just unfortunate as hell that the man had dropped from nowhere right into the middle of the plan.

"Thing is, we want him as a cover, The," Burlingame said now.

"I know that."

Elihu looked at the big man carefully. The trouble was, with that horrible face, you could never tell what he was thinking or feeling. He always looked angry. Not that Elihu cared. He had his orders, he knew the plan, and he was going to use anybody and everybody he could in the execution of his task. Praise the Lord!

Elihu Soames Burlingame, born Chuck Delaney, chuckled to himself now at how beautifully it was working out. Even to the point where he had begun to think and even, yes, feel like a reverend. And he was going to take advantage of that damn Slocum so unexpectedly turning up.

"So what now?" The was asking. "I ain't gonna wait forever 'fore I coldcock that Slocum sonofabitch."

"I understand, The. But things are moving now, and we should be reaching the call to action pretty soon."

"The sooner the quicker," observed The, who was a man not without a philosophical—if homey—cast of mind.

"Now, I want to be sure," Burlingame said, in a new tone of voice. "I want to be sure that nobody suspects anything."

The snorted. "Why would they, for Christ sake! You think I'm a fuckin' dumbbell or somethin'?"

Burlingame positively refused to answer that question, and waited a moment to control his irritation at The's surliness and stupidity. Then he said calmly, "The, I am only urging caution. We are into a big thing, and it would be stupid—very stupid, because very dangerous for the person it might involve—for anything unexpected to take place. Like somebody finding out that you and I are working together, or that you and I each came here separately for a particular purpose." And he wanted to add, but didn't, because The didn't know it, that they were also connected with Kitchen.

"You're saying we come here for some reason, huh?"

"I don't know how I could have put it more plainly," Elihu said, and this time he had a really hard time controlling himself.

"Well, what reason?"

"The, you are getting paid not to worry about it, and to just do as I tell you."

"So I done what you told me. I come here a whole couple months afore you, an' I got a saloon going, and I even hired some girls, like that fucking bitch what started the trouble with Slocum. She told me she'd handle the girls, be the madam, see. The damn bitch doesn't put out herself, though. How do you like that shit, huh?"

The Allen was very indignant at the thought of how Nellie was "wasting it," as he kept telling people. Yet, he had to admit she was good at handling the girls and keeping accounts. He hadn't really thought she'd been cheating him, like he'd claimed, it was only that he wanted to shake her some so he could get a chance in her pants. That bastard Slocum! Maybe he was after it too, by damn! Well, he would fix his fucking wheels next time—but good! He sat there furiously, with the air whistling out of his hairy nostrils.

Elihu Burlingame took out a cigar and lighted it, his thoughts on what the next development would be. Thus far, he had carried out his instructions to the letter. He took pride in that. He was a man who did his job, and did it one hundred percent. The trouble was when you had to work with fools it made life difficult. Men such as The, the big oaf. God, he could upset everything in a second. The man just had no sense. But there it was. There you were. You had to take what you were given in this best of all possible worlds. And this particular event was worth the difficulty. He'd end up rich as Croesus, whoever that was. Some old bugger in the Bible or someplace, he would have wagered. Elihu, though often evangelical in his manner, had never mastered the minutiae of his present professed calling. He was not one to fiddle with the detail of the past. Dates and other niceties of history bored him. What he reveled in, on the other hand, was the detail in the present. Such as the plan. He lived the plan. Indeed, it was himself who had been a major instrument in the execution of the plan. He took pride in that. And he hoped that the others did too. They should surely realize his importance.

The appearance of John Slocum had been a bad surprise. He had heard of Slocum, and his first reaction had been one of fear for the plan. A man like Slocum could easily become a major difficulty. But then he had thought of the possibility of using the man. He was a scout, a man of the trail. If they played it well, Slocum might turn up something useful. You never knew.

Elihu smiled. Yes, Slocum could be used. In the same way they would make use of Lord Frederick Edgerton and his visit to Little Missouri. True, it was Kyle who had thought up that basic part, Kyle who had worked it out after hearing of the English lord and his wish to visit the West—it had been in all the eastern papers—with references to the Grand Duke Alexis's hunting trip with Custer some years back and Sir George Gore's slaughtering of the buffalo and God knows how many other animals. Still, it was Elihu who had carried the mail, as it were; it was he who had been the mover in the action.

Filled with new importance, Elihu regarded his companion with fresh distaste. And as he sat there enjoying his cigar, he began to think about Lord Frederick and Lady Millecent. He was fully aware of the meeting between Three-Card Monte Kitchen and his companions with the English couple, though he didn't know the details. Yet, judging by the personnel accompanying Three-Card he had a pretty good idea of what was up. And when Lord Frederick had told him he wanted a buffalo hunt, and needed a guide, he'd suggested Slocum. An excellent way of keeping tabs on Slocum, and for that matter, the man might even turn up something that could be useful to the plan.

It was risky, for certain, because what if Slocum stumbled on something and found out what was really going on? On the other hand, Slocum might lead them right to the place. He felt a shiver go through him at the thought. By God, that sonofabitch Kyle had brass. He had balls, by God. Hell, the man had brass balls!

Meanwhile, let Three-Card and his boys also go their way. Though he did have kind of a sneaky feeling that Three-Card might already be working for Kyle. Kyle, damn it, was like that—coming at a caper from several angles, never just the one. And working people with some not knowing the others. Clever, but a real pain in the ass when the signals got crossed. Kyle did handle it, though. He sure had to hand it to him. Kyle, with all his irons in the fire.

The thrill shook him again. No doubt about it, that Kyle had brass nuts.

Slocum had told them the sad news, but it didn't seem to bother the English couple very much. He found them to be a little like children on a picnic; everything was of interest.

"My cousin Edward told me there were thousands of buffalo extant," Lord Frederick repeated. "It's hard to believe what you are now telling me." Yet there was no complaint in his voice.

"Take it or leave it," Slocum said amiably, smiling at Lady Millecent. He wasn't sure, but he could almost bet he saw a twinkle in her noble eye. "We can still go looking."

"It must be true, Frederick," she said, touching her husband's arm in the way she would touch a child. "Mr. Slocum obviously knows what he is talking about. Those other gentlemen . . ."

"Kitchen and his lot? Well, they said they looked and looked, and only came up with a couple or possibly three dozen scattered beasts. Maybe they didn't look in the right places."

"Yet they told you you could hunt," Lady Millecent insisted. "And Mr. Slocum, I believe, is saying that too."

"Well, I could hunt those couple of dozen, I suppose."

"But what happened to the buffalo?" the lady asked, turning to Slocum. "Cousin Edward said there were so many." She smiled suddenly, a very light smile. "And, since after all we *are* in America, please call me Millecent."

"And Frederick," added the Lord. "And may we call you John?"

"I reckon it wouldn't do any harm."

"Edward said you couldn't miss, the herds were so thick. You simply couldn't help hitting something."

Lady Millecent was in complete good humor, and not at all disappointed at the news Slocum had brought.

"What explanation did they give you?" Slocum asked. "I mean, why the buffalo had disappeared."

"Mr. Kitchen put forth the interesting explanation that during the spring the Sioux Indians must have driven the large herds to their reservation in the far north."

Slocum had difficulty controlling a smile at this piece of nonsense. But he held his tongue and said simply, "Anyway, the point is, there are hardly any buffalo left. Some people say it's because the hide hunters killed them. But however you slice it, they're not about to about." And he felt himself smiling at the adorable-looking Englishwoman. Yes, he was certain now— there was a twinkle.

"But we can still go hunting," insisted Lord Frederick. "I mean, I cannot possibly return home without some buffalo trophies."

"No problem," Slocum said easily. "It might take a bit to find something worth throwing down on, but we'll take a crack at 'er."

"When can we start?" Lord Frederick was all smiles at the prospect of his first buffalo kill.

"Tomorrow."

"When?"

He was like a little boy, Slocum thought. You couldn't help liking the fellow. And, as for his wife, you couldn't help all kinds of things. "About an hour before dawn," he said now. "Uh, will you be going along?" And his eyes had swung to the lady.

"But of course," said her husband. "Of course. Just tell me what we will need and we shall be ready."

He was as eager as any young boy going on an adventure—a young man not yet thirty, Slocum reckoned. And she, she was younger—in years, but certainly older in maturity.

He stayed with them another hour, telling them what supplies would be needed, that they would need packhorses besides their saddle animals, and suggested that Kitchen and his friends be put to work getting together the necessary gear and animals, plus two skinners, since Lord Frederick was already carrying them on his payroll for such services.

Then he checked their rifles. Both told him they had done a lot of target shooting, and he could see by the way the young woman handled her Sharps that she knew what she was doing.

"Have you ever hunted any wild game before?" he asked her.

She shook her head. "Ducks. A deer. But I didn't like shooting the deer. I don't know if I will wish to kill a buffalo. If he is nice-looking, I won't." And she looked at him with her bright hazel eyes very wide. He found her absolutely tantalizing, and he wondered how much of her manner was for him and if she was that way with everybody. He'd never met an English noblewoman before, but it didn't bother him. Hell, he had met, and he had known, a helluva lot of women.

"But I thought we were going to ride our horses after the buffalo and shoot them at close range," Millecent was saying as they sat over their first campfire.

They had left Little Muddy early that morning accompanied by two skinners, furnished by Three-Card and his colleagues, and had ridden all day without seeing a single buffalo. Now they had made camp near a great butte on the south fork of Wood River.

Slocum smiled at the young woman's words. "That's the way the writers back east tell it," he said. "And the artists—a lot of them paint the Indians riding down the buffs and dropping them with bow and arrow or even a handgun. But that's rare."

"You mean, that's all poppycock," Frederick said. "I am not surprised. Those scriveners in the East, and back home, too, are not at all to be relied upon." He got up from his cross-legged position, reached over for the coffeepot, and poured.

"The buff hunters consider that fancy-Dan stuff when the whites do it, using a handgun up close," Slocum explained. "The old-timers, they don't consider that serious hunting. You have to have a trained horse for it, plus it scatters the carcasses all over the place, making it tough on the skinners. And besides all that, it stampedes the herd. Course it's different when the Indians do it. They know what they're doing."

"So what is the right way, then?" Millecent asked.

"Well, the real buff hunter, he stalks the herd, see, till he gets within a few hundred yards, and then he sets about making one-shot kills."

Slocum accepted another refill of coffee at that point, and also one of Frederick's great cigars.

"See, you've got the right guns. Somebody told you right. Some buff hunters work with both a .40-70 and a .40-90. But you know, everybody has his favorite."

"What's yours, John?" Millecent asked.

He took a pull on his coffee. "I favor that big Sharps there in my scabbard. It's a .69 caliber, single shot, and I generally use a tripod; it's got linen cartridges."

"Edward—my cousin—spoke of shooting from a prone position," Frederick said.

"That puts the muzzle only a few inches from the ground," Slocum said. "The trouble with that is the reverberation of the shot likely might frighten the buffs. It's better to keep your muzzle well off the ground."

He stood up suddenly and walked to his bedding and warbag. In a moment he was back.

"These here are buffalo sticks," he explained, holding the pair of sticks so they could see them clearly in the firelight. "These are made of bois d'arc; sometimes they call it Osage orange."

The sticks were almost three feet long, and they were riveted together near one end, but not so tightly that they wouldn't swing open like a pair of shears, as he now demonstrated.

"See, you put the barrel of your rifle in the upper crotch and you hold both sticks and the barrel with your left hand."

"Provided you happen to be right-handed," Millecent said. "I happen to be left-handed."

"Well, then you hold it with your left foot," Slocum said. And the three of them had a good laugh.

They talked some more, Slocum telling them how the skinners came after the buff hunters and were paid around 25 cents for getting the hide off a buffalo and pegging it out to dry.

"Sounds like hard work," Frederick said. "It sounds like nasty work."

"Heard of a feller named John Cook," Slocum told them, "who is supposed to have skinned 902 buffalo in 42 days. That's an average of twenty-two animals a day."

"Nasty work," said Lord Frederick again, shaking his head wryly.

"The wolfers come after," Slocum said, going on with his story.

"I know who they are," Lady Millecent said. "They kill the wolves."

"Right." Slocum looked over at Lord Frederick. "You think the buff hunters are rough, tough, and feisty. A wolfer is rougher, tougher, and feistier."

"Do you think we'll find buffalo tomorrow?" the Englishman asked as they stood up to go to bed.

"Might."

"And if we don't find them tomorrow, we'll find them the next day," his wife said. "Right?" And she raised her forehead questioningly as she looked at Slocum.

"Right."

"Good night."

"Night," Slocum said, and, without taking another look at her, he walked out to his bedroll, and within minutes he was inside it with his six-gun handy, and his thoughts on how they were camped, where, and what possibility there might be of an enemy coming upon them in the night.

He didn't go to sleep for a while. He knew that something was bothering him, and lying there, he reviewed the evening, and back into the day, too, to see if there was something that would reveal why he felt as he did.

He could find nothing. Whatever it was, though, would not let him go. Finally, when he was sure his two companions were asleep, he got up and scouted around the campsite. He found nothing that satisfied the feeling that was growing inside him.

Or was it the girl? he asked himself. He was certainly taken with her. She was special. But no, this particular feeling wasn't sexual in any way. It was the feeling of near danger. It was his blood talking to him. His Cherokee blood.

4

It was getting to be like the Chinese boxes that children played with, Elihu Burlingame was thinking. He had to keep a cool head. Alert. Sharp. This was essential, or things could get mixed up. Kyle, of course, was always throwing in new elements—another angle here, another facet there. Just like in the riverboat game when they'd taken that whole damn boatload of card mechanics. God, that had been something! But, like now, there had been so many elements, and most of them things that Kyle had thrown in to confuse their quarry. In the action that time in Denver, too. And, hell, he could go on. The point was that right now, it was hard to keep track, what with all the people involved: himself and his wagonload of so-called immigrants, who wouldn't fool a blind man, and Lord Frederick Edgerton and his wife, and then Slocum right in the middle of it. And of course, not to forget the goddamn Indians, sitting right on the area in question. Maybe. Of course, only maybe. On account of nobody—not himself, not Kyle—was sure of just

47

where to look for the thing. But, shit, if the Injuns got
into it, the Army couldn't be far behind.

He had warned Kyle of this. And Kyle—smooth as a
washed pebble—had held up a soft hand, telling him
not to worry. The plan was all but foolproof. There was
in fact a contact who would, if necessary, handle the
Army. And with all the false trails Kyle was laying out,
they would have a clear way to their purpose.

"We will have a clear way to our purpose." Kyle had
indeed said those very words to him as they sat in Annie
Edward's cathouse in K.C. and made their final review.

"You will be the Reverend Elihu Soames Burlingame," Kyle had told him. "You are no longer Chuck
Delaney."

"Christ sakes, Kyle," Elihu had said—and he made
a definite point of calling himself Elihu in his thoughts,
the better to become his role. "For Christ sakes, I've
been so many names and things with you, pretty soon I
won't know who the hell I am!"

"Or care either, eh? Since you'll be so rich!" laughed
Kyle, his long, horselike face almost nickering as his
great teeth stuck out.

"Shit," Elihu had murmured.

"You just keep yourself sharp," Kyle had said. He
gazed into the middle distance. "The Reverend Elihu
Soames Burlingame. And don't ever forget the 'Reverend' part!"

"Why the hell such a fancy name?" Elihu had asked.

"Because names are important," Kyle had said.
"With a name like that, plus a title and all, a lot of
people won't dare question you."

Elihu had nodded, a smile coming into his face.
"You know, you're right, Kyle. They'll be questioning
the church, like."

"They'll be questioning God," Kyle had said. And taking out a pearl-handled penknife he'd started to pare his fingernails. "And of course, you'll have your wife and child with you. You know Myrtle. You met her in St. Jo. Remember? And you'll be married to her—her name is Charlotte, but you will affectionately call her Charlie."

"But what about the kid?" Elihu had asked, somewhat alarmed at the prospect of being responsible for a youngster. "How old is it?"

"It is a fourteen-year-old who will be playing the part of a ten-year-old girl. Her name is Dolly, but you will know her as Sarah. Remember, your daughter Sarah, ten years old."

"Jesus!" Elihu had almost hissed the word.

"Sarah," repeated Kyle.

"Kyle, where in hell do you get all these people for your action? How can I know this kid won't blow the whole thing? I mean, it's hard enough with grown-ups."

"Stop worrying," Kyle had said. "The kid will always be with Charlie. Get the name—Charlie! Charlie will not let Sarah out of her sight. Charlie's worked with her before."

"You're sure, Kyle?" He realized it was a dumb thing to say.

Kyle had smiled, not answering. Indeed, the corners of his mouth pulled way back, and his lips protruded along the tips of his big teeth: Just like a horse might smile, Elihu had thought. "This kid is good. I've used her before. Got her from Bemus in St. Louis. He's got three, four kids. Rents them out. And he's got adults, too. Like Myrtle. You need a schoolmarm? A housewife? A reverend?" And leaning over he gave Elihu a cute poke in the side with his elbow.

Elihu had to laugh at that. He did like Kyle. Kyle had it—whatever "it" was. He knew how to get you to do the damnedest things!

All this was running through his mind as he sat in the Stud nursing his beer. Yet at the same time he felt the worry. Who was that he had seen in the Sure Shot? And was it anyone who might maybe know him?

He stood up, suddenly thinking of Charlie. Yes, a good idea of Kyle's, having the child along. It gave the right tone to anyone questioning anything. An attractive wife, a child, not to forget a handsome man of God. And he chuckled to himself as he left the Stud.

Funny, he was thinking as he made his way out to where the Conestoga was set apart from the other wagons. Funny how when he was feeling like he was right now nothing else mattered a damn. The only problem was, though, what to do with the damn kid while he had at Charlie. For it wasn't anywhere near her bedtime. Well, maybe Charlie would think of a way. Maybe between the two of them, Charlie could think of a way. By God, he chuckled to himself, he wasn't getting all that much pay from Kyle and his pals, whoever the hell they were, but that he shouldn't have a little trade on the side!

There was no question but that even with the competition of The Allen's Stud, Packy O'Gatty's Sure Shot was still drawing a goodly count of clientele. That is to say, the drinkers and cardplayers and those interested in the dice, the wheel of fortune, and whenever there was a dealer handy, faro, all had a number of choices where they might exercise their talents.

Packy himself, a chunky individual with a knobby head, sharp elbows, and, when it came to dancing, a lively pair of legs, ran the whole shebang, even tending bar—though not always from the sober side. But at the moment Mr. O'Gatty had left the bar in the care of his right-hand man, Harelip Schneider, a man of advanced years, yet a man quick with a bung starter and short on morality when trouble arose. Harelip was good at keeping order, in other words.

At the moment Harelip was staring at the stranger who had appeared at the bar and asked for whiskey. He thought he had seen that face before, but he couldn't place it. Denver was it? K.C.? It didn't come, and there was no time to stand gawking over it. Well, a man couldn't remember everybody he'd dealt a drink or for that matter a card to. The West was one helluva big place. Maybe . . . No, he must be mistaken.

Meanwhile, under a thick cloud of smoke in the back room of the Sure Shot a group of earnest players were seated at a round table, their heads bent in concentration. The game was jacks or better, and the players were those six who had visited the conveyance and offered their services to Lord Frederick in his wished-for buffalo hunt. Only to be aced out, as Three-Card Monte Kitchen had put it, by the man named Slocum, the one who had beat up on The Allen, by God, and looked to be no man to get previous with over anything at all.

It was Three-Card's deal. Accepting the deck, he released a harsh sigh, and, leaning his elbows on the table, he fanned open the deck of cards with one hand as he held it at eye level.

"You know, it was the Gypsies who invented the deck of cards, my friends," he said. At that point a sudden cough wracked him, and he turned purple in the face and dropped the cards.

"Damn! Damnation!" he coughed out between sneezing and spluttering and hacking. "Damn it to hell! Man gets on in years an' he loses, by God, a man *loses*!" Finally he controlled himself, with the help of the two men on either side of him, who slapped him on the back and poured whiskey into his glass. Subsiding, he reached for the cards, folded them into a deck, cut, shuffled, cut again, and began to deal. Meanwhile, low laughter and merry chatter had supported the moment. The boys were enjoying themselves.

"They ain't gonna find enough buffalo out there to put a robe on one of them Sioux dolls," Elbows McFadden said knowingly.

"That Slocum'll slicker 'em, an' that's a gut," put in Cy Pone. "Time they git back to here they'll be glad to deal with us, eh, Monte?"

Three-Card grinned. Actually he was grinning at the pair of aces he had dealt himself following his coughing attack, which had served to distract his companions.

"Now we got to figure somethin' we can do to separate His Lordship from his money bags. Wouldn't you say yes to that, boys?" And Three-Card's grin broadened.

"Sure would!" Bill Forefinger, who ran the livery in Little Misery, nodded his hairy face.

"Ante a dollar," Three-Card said now, after the hand had closed with himself raking in the winnings. And he reached for a fresh deck. It was a deck he had worked on only the day before, so that he could read the cards from their backs, thanks to the tiny pinpricks he had inserted at strategic places.

Nobody objected to the dollar ante, and the money was put into the pot.

"I pass," said Clem Abernathy, and clamped his jaws hard on his short cigar.

Bill Forefinger opened. "I'll make it a dollar for opening. And by God, we're playing for real money, boys! Don't that feel good!"

"It's a change," Three-Card said sourly.

"Looks like I'm in," Cy Pone said, and he took a drink from the glass at his elbow.

Three-Card Kitchen watched his cards and chewed on his cold stogie.

Elbows McFadden tossed in a silver dollar.

"Dealer stays," Three-Card said, keeping his eyes straight on his cards.

Clem Abernathy pushed in a dollar and drew two cards.

"I'll take a card," said Packy O'Gatty.

"Three," Cy Pone said. He looked at the three cards Three-Card dealt, and tossed them into the discard. Sniffing, he ran the back of his hand across his red nose and settled back into his chair, scratching his crotch with sudden vigor.

Bill Forefinger belched softly into his cards as he examined them minutely. "Ought to pass, I ought. But, hell take it, I'll bet five."

Clem Abernathy shoved five cartwheels into the pot. "Make it another five," he said.

Bill Forefinger grinned, and scratched the side of his face.

"I pass," said Elbows.

"I'll make it another five, by golly," said Bill Forefinger.

Three-Card's voice was soft as he said, "I'll call."

"I call your five and raise you five more," Clem Abernathy said.

Bill Forefinger focused tightly on his cards, which he

was gripping so hard they curved. "See you and raise you five," he said.

It was then that Three-Card Monte said, "I call, and raise another ten dollars."

Bill Forefinger's jaw dropped to his chest, while total astonishment swept into the other player's faces.

"Shit on a shingle! Falling for that one! By God, I'll bet my ass you got four of a kind there, Three-Card!"

"There's a way to verify it," Three-Card said slyly, grinning inside at his sharp caper in letting the last bet go by.

"We'll soon enough see," Abernathy said, grim as an undertaker. "Forefinger! What you say there!"

"I'm in. Let's have a look." He leaned forward eagerly.

Chuckling all the way from deep in his throat, Three-Card laid down four queens and an ace and pulled in the sizable pot.

"Boys, I am buyin' the round."

At that precise moment the door opened and Harelip Schneider entered.

"There is a feller"—with his large eyes on Packy O'Gatty, he nodded in the general direction from which he had come—"looks to be a lawman. Only I can't fix him. I ain't sure. Thought I better tell you, boss."

Six totally innocent faces greeted this remark of Harelip's. Hands were opened in guiltless offering. Eyes glazed with guileless ignorance looked into endless space.

"Just thought I better tell it," said Harelip, suddenly feeling guilty of some unspeakable crime. "You men ready for drinks?"

"On me," Three-Card said.

Packy, returned to his role of owner of the Sure Shot,

followed Harelip out. In a moment or two he was back, his companions having waited in chaste silence the while. "Not someone of any account, far as I can tell," was the succinct report.

"Ever see him before?" asked Cy Pone.

"Never. Could be the law. But there is people in this town—I mean, I bin told—who now and again toss a wide loop. I mean, if you know what I mean."

This observation brought a cute round of laughter from all. They were ready for their drinks when Harelip returned with a fresh bottle.

When the door had closed behind him, Three-Card said, "We got to get going on our new plan. Got to keep His Lordship feeding us in the style we'd like to be more familiar with, eh boys?"

"Tell the plan," Elbows said. "I ain't any too clear on it. And anyways, that Slocum feller slipped in there ahead of us on the buff hunting. I thought you was going to hire him and then rent him to His Lordship, Three-Card."

"Slocum ain't the kind of feller you rent," Three-Card said, his sour words bringing a pause into their midst.

"Could be Slocum will be having himself something lined up by now with His Lordship," Bill Forefinger said. "Or leastways by the time they get done with their buff hunting."

A silence fell briefly as Three-Card reached for the bottle and poured himself an ample amount. "No, we're set now, I think. Lord Frederick'll have his buffalo hunt. I know Slocum will get him something, though it could take some little time. Then when he gets back we'll have our project ready. I talked it over with him."

"With Lord Frederick?" said Cy Pone.

Three-Card took a drink, and came up gasping for air. "My, that is wicked stuff!" He cleared his throat. "Now see, what we got to do is build a abbatoir."

"A what?"

"A abbatoir. It's a slaughterhouse."

"Then whyn't you say so!"

"I just did."

"You didn't. You said abba . . . abbat . . . whatever the hell you said!"

Considering the amount of alcohol the group had consumed, Three-Card showed remarkable restraint. His voice was even as he resumed his speech. "We got to build a slaughterhouse. I was using His Lordship's word, you dumb shit! Now then—"

"What do we want a slaughterhouse for?"

"It'll be instead of shipping cattle on the hoof, live beef—got it?—from the range out here all the way to Chicago for slaughtering. The animals can just as easy be slaughtered right here in the middle of range country, at Little Muddy here."

"Jesus!"

"It'll be cheaper, easier to ship dressed beef than beef on the hoof like all those dumb cattle outfits been doing. And besides, a lot of it which would be sold west of Chicago wouldn't have to make the round trip. You got it, you dumb shithead?"

"Jesus!" someone said again. It was Bill Forefinger. "That sounds like one helluva idee! I am for it! Let's get to work on it. I mean, building that 'abbat' thing—the slaughterhouse."

Clem Abernathy, who hadn't drunk quite as much as his companions, though he had not been niggardly with his intake either, now stood up and emitted a wet chuckle from deep in his throat. "Boys, I got to get to work. Told Elmer I'd take the night shift at the hotel. Just know that I'm in on it—whatever the hell you call the damn thing!"

"It ain't exactly what you'd call a great big herd," Slocum said as he watched the huge animals grazing only a few hundred yards away.

"Is this where we'll shoot them?" Lady Millecent asked. "From here?"

"That's right. We're downwind of them, a good three hundred yards," Slocum pointed out. He had kept his eyes on the buffalo as he spoke. There were some thirty or so animals in the herd; certainly it was small. But he felt lucky to have found this many. It was enough for their purpose. Both Lord Frederick and Lady Millecent were thrilled, as far as he could see.

"When can we shoot?" Lord Frederick asked eagerly. "I want first shot, Millecent," he said.

"Of course, my lord and master, of course!" And she gave a sly wink to Slocum, which brought a shout of delighted laughter from Frederick.

"What a creature, my wife—eh? Don't you think so, John?"

"I sure do," Slocum said, with his eyes still on the herd. Yet he was finding it difficult to keep his thoughts away from the girl and firmly on the business at hand.

"But what if the herd stampedes?" Lord Frederick asked suddenly. "What if it stampedes toward *us*?" And Slocum was interested to hear more excitement than alarm in the nobleman's voice. He liked him.

"We're after one-shot kills," he explained. "That should hold them." He nodded toward the pair of bay packhorses they had brought along. "Let's unload and get ready." He was looking at the two men they had hired for skinners. They were standing off to one side, their eyes casually on the three, who were now moving toward the two packhorses.

"You men keep well back," Slocum called out. "We don't want them moving. I'm going to shoot a cow first off, so they won't stampede."

The two skinners said nothing, but continued to stand where they were, not offering to help with unloading the packhorses.

Slocum was examining Lord Frederick's rifle. It was a big weapon, a .50-70 Sharps, with a telescope sight made by Vollmer of Jena, Germany. Expensive. Besides the rifle there was a bullet mold, a tool for decapping and recapping the brass shells, a swage for resizing the shells, and a bullet seater. Slocum knew it cost plenty; and the telescope sight was at least an additional seventy-five to eighty dollars. As well as the usual cross hairs, the scope reticle had two additional horizontal cross hairs, like the stadia hairs in a surveyor's transit. Slocum knew—having used a similar weapon—that when the rifle was sighted to hit the bull's-eye at two hundred yards, using the intersection of the uppermost cross-hair and the vertical cross hair, a shot aimed with the next lower cross hair went fifteen inches high, and with the lowest the bullet went thirty inches high. It took a fine judge of distance to figure which cross hairs to use out beyond two hundred yards.

"I'll take the first shot," Slocum said, opening his buffalo sticks.

"I thought sometimes people lay down to shoot," Lady Millecent said.

"That's not a good idea, at least not for us now. See, they'll feel the vibration running along the ground and they could stampede. I want the muzzle high up. I'll be kneeling. I do believe I told you that already."

She blushed furiously. "I—I forgot!"

He grinned at her. Then he knelt on one knee and put the barrel of the Sharps in the upper crotch of the buffalo sticks, while he held the sticks with his left hand.

"What do you figure is the distance?" he asked his companions.

"I'd say two hundred yards," Lord Frederick said immediately.

"Four hundred," Lady Millecent said after a short pause.

"It's three," Slocum said. He stood up. "I need to be closer to them."

"Won't they see you?" Lady Millecent asked.

"They're very nearsighted," he said. He had not taken his eyes off the animals, and kept watching them closely as he repositioned himself. "They can't see us, and because we're downwind they can't smell us."

"What do you think of the quality of those hides?" Lord Frederick suddenly asked.

"You won't find any silks in that bunch," Slocum said, deciding to tell the bare truth. "But there might be a fair decent hide or two. We'll do our best."

"I take it by silks you mean the top grade," Lady Millecent said.

Slocum didn't answer. He had set up his buffalo sticks again at about two hundred yards from the grazing herd. He laid the barrel of his Sharps on the sticks. Taking careful aim, he squeezed off a shot, holding for the lungs of an old cow. He watched the impact of the bullet. The cow, as he had known she would, kept her feet and began to bleed.

"You missed," said Lady Millecent.

"Now you watch. Just watch and don't talk so much."

He felt her tighten—she was standing close to him. But he didn't mind; it was time the two of them learned a thing or two, he decided.

Slocum was watching the herd carefully. The other buffalo, now smelling the blood, began to mill around the wounded cow.

"Clever," said Lord Frederick behind him. "I see your strategy there, my man. Capital!"

Slocum bent to the Sharps, aimed, and squeezed. This time he was aiming at the neck of a bull. It was a clean shot, the big animal dropped right where he stood.

"That one'll be mine," he said, and he stood up.

"I didn't know you wanted to shoot one," Frederick said. "I don't know why, but I had that feeling."

"I shot it for two reasons. One, to show you how to do it without stampeding the whole herd. And two..." He stopped, squinted at the sun, and said, "Better get going. Weather's likely to change some, and it is getting late in the day."

"Millecent, let me go first," her husband said.

"That we already decided, my dear." She turned all at once on Slocum. "What was the second reason you wanted to shoot? You were going to tell us."

He looked at her. "Sometimes there's Indians about. I've heard there's a tribe of Arapaho near Little Misery —not too close, but close enough to be neighbor. Sometimes they like to get some buff meat, especially the tongue; and they can always use an extra hide."

They were both good shots, though Lady Millecent missed her first try. But she got her buffalo on the second shot. Lord Frederick got his on his first. He was delighted. When Slocum saw how excited he was at his

success he wondered whether his wife had maybe
missed her first shot on purpose.

Without a sound evening had entered the sky, and
then night came softly, and yet with its unique same-
ness—the repetition that made it—like the dawn—so
special.

A coyote barked. Some animal rustled inside the
timberline. And a gentle wind brought fresh smells to
the three seated around the campfire.

They had eaten well, and Lord Frederick had pro-
duced a fine bottle of Armagnac brandy. In the nick of
time Slocum had stopped him from offering it to the
skinners, who had made their camp some distance away.

"Just wishing to be hospitable, old boy," Lord Frederick said, chagrined that Slocum had blocked his gen-
erosity.

"They've got liquor already," Slocum told him. "You
don't want them drinking. They're not all that reliable
anyway."

"But I got them through that funny man—Two-Card
something or other."

"Three-Card," his wife interjected. "The fast-talking
man."

"Do you know where he got them from?" Slocum
asked.

"I have no idea," Lord Frederick said. He was obviously still put out. "Well, I see I really don't know
Westerners yet." And he threw out a little laugh, aimed
obviously at himself.

At this point Lady Millecent came in with instant
salve. "Darling, everything takes time. I'm sure John's
right in his decision. After all, we have agreed to put
ourselves in his hands."

"Oh, I wasn't questioning John!" The alarm was quite evident in his voice.

And they all laughed at that, relieving the moment that Frederick's tension had brought.

"I must admit," Lady Millecent said. "Those men are, well, not people you would meet at a ball. In point of fact, I can see how they might become somewhat frightening."

"But . . ." Frederick expostulated, staring at his beautiful wife. "They wouldn't dare . . . What?" he asked himself. "They wouldn't dare take, well, liberties. They are servants, after all. I mean to say. . . ."

"I'm keeping an eye on them," Slocum said. "There's nothing to worry about. Skinners, wolfers— they're a rough lot. That's the way they live."

"I've been wondering about something," Lord Frederick said after a short silence.

"What, darling?" Lady Millecent looked suddenly at Slocum and smiled, as though encouraging him to speak.

It was so clear to Slocum now how she pampered her husband. Even so, he had a feeling that Lord Frederick had a definite mind of his own, and very likely took advantage of his wife's attitude. Anyhow, with a woman as attractive as Lady Millecent, who could care about much else in the way of small habits or attitudes? And it wasn't just her looks, he told himself, nor the fact that she was so extremely sensuous. For she had a great energy. It was compelling. He wondered whether it was irresistible for Lord Frederick. And the thought surprised him.

"What were you wondering, Freddie?" Millecent

asked again, as the Englishman seemed to be lost in thought.

"I was thinking of Uncle Harry." He turned toward Slocum. "Uncle Harry, as I may have said, was here some years ago. He was killed by the Indians."

"Here?" Slocum asked. "Right around here?"

"I believe so. I am not all that certain. It was a good while ago, and my cousin Edward told me something about it. But then Edward got ill and died. Suddenly. I wanted to come here, where Uncle Harry had been. He loved it. And I've always thought it unfortunate that his body was sent back to England. I feel sure he would have wanted to be buried here."

A strange silence fell over the campfire then. Or so Slocum felt. Strange, he thought, this young man and his wife coming out here where his uncle had visited long ago.

"Do you know what tribe it was that did him in?"

"I've no idea. Whatever tribe is around here, I suppose."

"Shoshone and Arapaho mostly. But that doesn't mean they were here then. The tribes move around, and now they get moved around by the government."

"Uncle Harry must have loved it here," Lady Millecent said. "I mean, I never met him, but I've heard he was a sort of poet. He wrote some poetry, it seems."

"He was a good poet. My father told me." Lord Frederick seemed to be thinking of something.

"What did he do for a living?" Slocum asked. "Or didn't he have to work?" He said this with a smile, which his two companions picked up.

"Oh, he had to work," Lord Frederick said. "He wasn't like the rest of the family. He was poor. He ran away from home, he went to sea, he did all kinds of things."

"He came here to this beautiful country," Lady Millecent said.

"Well," said Slocum. "It's too bad he was killed. I take it he died young."

"Yes. Young." Lord Frederick's furrowed brow suddenly cleared. "It may sound strange to you two, but I have had a notion growing in me. I . . . for the life of me I can't say why, but I'd like to visit his grave. I shall have to ask around to see if anybody remembers it."

"But I thought you said he was buried in England?" Slocum said.

"Yes, he was buried in England—finally. But first he was buried somewhere around here."

"You mean, then they dug him up and sent his body back to England?"

Lady Millecent said, "It was all a legal business. The family wanted his body home, but they had to get somebody to come over here and make the arrangements. A lot of legal business to go through, taking up everybody's time and a good deal of money, which, as far as I could tell, no one minded."

Slocum said nothing to all this.

After a moment Lord Frederick said, "No need to bore you with all this family detail, John. Maybe it's time to turn in, eh?" And he stood up.

Slocum suddenly had an idea. "Did your uncle own any property here?"

"Not that I know of. As I said, he was not a rich man. More on the poor side, which he preferred. Mind you, he was a lovely man. Everyone loved him, especially children. Actually, he was rather like a child himself. I remember how he used to tell us—he was my father's only brother, by the way, and younger—anyway, he used to tell us children—I have three brothers and two sisters—he used to tell us how he was looking for a gold mine. You see, we were always asking him about his adventures, why he was always away from home and so on. And of course, when he did come home we always monopolized him; we always asked him if he'd found his gold mine yet."

"I heard he always brought you fabulous gifts," Lady Millecent said.

"Indeed he did, even though they weren't always expensive gifts. If he had the money they were, but more often than not they were strange things from strange lands." Lord Frederick paused, searching his memory. "I was very touched—I believe we all were—when we received his last letter. Not so incidentally, he wrote beautiful letters; you felt you were actually in the place where he was. Anyway, in his last letter I was so touched when he said that at last he'd found his gold mine."

"Did he tell you where?" Slocum said with a smile.

"He meant the gold mine in the sky he'd always told us he was looking for."

"I know. I understood that."

"Maybe he found a beautiful woman," Lady Millecent said. "I understand he was a very handsome man."

"Well, a beautiful woman is in fact a gold mine," Slocum replied. "And very likely even better."

And on that pleasant note their evening ended, and they stood up and went off to bed.

Slocum walked to the timberline, where he had thrown his bedroll, just inside the line of spruce which offered him good protection. He lay down.

He waited a few moments, thinking over the evening he had spent with Lord Frederick and Lady Millecent. After a while he rose and started to make a wide circle around the camp.

5

"Kyle didn't say you were part of the deal, my friend, and the quicker you understand the better!"

She stood facing him, her head just touching the canvas top of the Conestoga wagon, while he remained seated on his bedroll. His knees were drawn up, and he had his arms hanging over them as he arched his eyes up to her, covering her firm body beneath her tight dress, and finally resting on her angry face.

"Hell, you don't have to get so uppity. I been holding it in all this way out here, and by God I don't allow that I can stand it anymore. I mean, I got to have it!"

"I'm not interested. I made that plain when we started, damn you, Elihu! And I want you to understand it right now. Look, we're into a big thing here. I can feel it. And we don't want to mess it up now."

"Course not! You think I'm dumb, fer Christ sake!"

"Then keep your hands to yourself!" she snapped, and started to move toward the opening at the rear of the wagon.

"Where are you going?"

"That's none of your business."

"Slocum isn't about."

"So what?"

"I seen the eyes you've got for him. You can't hide that kind of thing. Listen, Charlie, c'mon. I can give you as good a time as any man. Better! What the hell, why not give me a try?"

"Why don't you go and get a girl? Hell, you brought those two along on the trip, and they seem to be making out all right in town."

"They're not what I want. I want you."

"Sorry, mister." She was at the opening at the end-gate of the wagon. "And let's not have any more of this. I told you last time, and the time before. No. N-o. No!"

"Let's have a drink then," he said in a new voice. "I got some good whiskey from The Allen. He brings in good stuff. Here." He reached for the bottle near his bedding, as he felt her hesitation. He knew her weakness.

"I'll take a short one," she said. "Just a couple of fingers. I've got to meet one of the old ladies about starting a school."

"Like this, huh?" And he held out his index and middle finger, spread wide apart.

"Like this," she said with a sharp laugh, and held up the same fingers but close together.

"We'll compromise," he said, pouring into her glass. Handing it to her he said, "Relax. I won't bother you. Sit. We need to talk things over. I mean, about business."

"I'm sorry, Chuck. I just don't—"

"Forget it," he snapped. "And damn it, the name is Elihu!"

She had seated herself on a crate opposite his bedroll and now took a pull at her drink, chastened at his reminding her of Kyle's firm instructions about names and roles.

"Good, isn't it?" he said after he had done the same. And he sighed.

She smiled a careful smile then. "Don't think you're going to get me drunk, Elihu, because you're not."

"I wouldn't dream of such a thing. After all, a man of God, as we all know, must be absolutely firm in his denial of carnal strivings. Right now, my dear, I am thinking of money."

"Money?"

"Big money. I mean, like gold."

"Gold!"

Elihu grinned at her. "I might let you in on my thoughts, but first I want to just relax a little. I've had a long day, my dear ... wife." And he leaned back, chuckling at some private joke.

Charlie watched him, wondering what he was up to. She had known him over the years, had worked with him before, the time they'd salted part of a desert with diamonds and pulled a real killing on some big fish— San Francisco bankers and a New York man, too. Kyle had worked that one beautifully. But right now, she hadn't a notion what the present action was leading to. It seemed that Chuck Delaney—the Reverend Burlingame—had some idea. And she was burning with curiosity.

At the same time, she knew she wouldn't be able to stand the man touching her. He had tried a few times, but she didn't like him. That other fellow, Slocum, now that was something else. She would have liked that.

Carefully she studied the man across from her as she took another drink. And she told herself she had better be careful not to drink too much. Especially now.

He had left the immediate area of the camp he was sharing with the English couple to make his evening rounds. He smelled the skinners as soon as he reached the open area where he had picketed the horses. They smelled stronger than the horses. Now, as he came closer to their camp, he could hear their voices. They were making no attempt to be careful, as he had warned them. Likely they'd been drinking, he reasoned. The damn fools. At the same time, it could work to his advantage. In fact, he came up almost close enough to touch one of them, who was sitting with his back to the line of trees that served Slocum as cover.

The other man was facing Slocum but couldn't see him, for the foliage was thick and it was nighttime. The two figures were well outlined in the light of the fire at which they were sitting.

"Anyways, that's what the man said." These words came from the skinner facing Slocum. His name was Cooch, and he spoke with a French accent. He was a stocky little brute with big knuckles on his hands, and he had a wild beard through which his red face showed itself in the firelight.

His companion spat angrily into the fire, then, leaning, he placed his thumb alongside his nose and blew in the same direction, though not with equal accuracy, some getting on his trouser leg.

"Shit!"

Slocum wasn't sure whether the epithet was in response to Cooch's remark or to the poor aim he had just shown. In any case, it was greeted with a moment of silence.

Slocum remembered Cooch from the wagon train. He had heard someone call him by name. He wasn't sure of the other man. He could have been in Elihu's train or not. It didn't matter.

"Emil," Cooch suddenly said. "Cut the shit and tell me what the hell's going on?"

Emil shrugged, tapped his forehead with two fingers, released a great sigh. "How the hell should I know? I know nothing. You know more than me. You just said something I didn't know, Cooch."

"About the man."

"What you heard."

"I jus' tell you what he said. That is all Cooch know."

They were drinking, and Slocum had the impulse to walk in and blast them for disobeying his orders. But he didn't. First of all he didn't want them to know he was around, and second he did want to hear anything they might have to say of interest.

But they sat in silence, no longer returning to the man they had mentioned, or what he had said.

He waited. He had the distinct feeling that the two men, Cooch and Emil, were not along only for the buffalo hunt, but that they would report the whole action to Elihu Burlingame.

But why? Why would Burlingame be so interested in the buffalo hunt? Who was Elihu anyway? Slocum was pretty sure by now that he was a con man. Obviously there was a game going on, and Lord Frederick was the target, the greener. Money, of course. But in what way? How were the cards being dealt? Was Elihu running a swindle? Or was there somebody in back of Elihu?

Why had the wagon train come to Little Misery in the first place? And with those particular travelers? Something was being set up—that was as plain as the stink made by Cooch and Emil. By God, they smelled like skinners, they looked like skinners, they stank like skinners. No question—they were skinners. And they were up to something—or someone was—with a different kind of stink.

He decided not to interrupt them. Cooch was dozing, and though he couldn't see Emil as clearly, he thought he saw his head nodding. Well then, it was time to leave.

That decision had hardly formed itself when he heard the branch crack, and he froze.

He waited, his whole body listening. A moment passed. Another. Nothing. The sound had come from off to his right. Hardly breathing now, he changed his position and began to move in the opposite direction from the sound. He moved in absolute silence, now and again stopping to listen.

Then he heard it again, coming from the same direction. Something, a branch, rustling. Keeping well under cover now, he moved toward the sound, completing his semicircle to the edge of a small meadow.

The moon had come out from behind a bank of cloud, and the clearing was well lighted. A man was standing next to a horse, checking the animal's rigging prior to mounting. He lifted the stirrup strap and laid it on his shoulder as he tightened the cinch. The horse stood well, a cow pony who appeared to Slocum to have been well broken. The man and the horse were not far from the line of trees in which Slocum was standing watching them.

As the man took the reins in his hand and gathered a handful of the horse's mane at the same time, Slocum pegged him as young. Slocum moved now right to the very edge of the trees, measuring the distance, and as the man lifted his leg to step into the stirrup he charged.

The man was taken completely by surprise as Slocum's arm snaked around his neck, clinching his throat and shutting off his breath, while at the same time a fist hard as a ramrod slammed into his lower back. His air was cut off by his attacker's forearm and so he couldn't make a sound, not even a grunt. And then Slocum had him on the ground with a knee in his throat.

"You make a sound you're dead," he snapped. And he had his Colt out now with the barrel pushing right into the prone man's forehead.

It was clearly impossible for the man to make any sound at all, but as Slocum released the pressure on his throat his breath came in little rushes of relief.

"You hear me! Whisper!"

"Yeah . . . yeah, I hear you."

"Now we're going to get up very slowly, without making any noise, and you're going to tell me what you're doing here."

Slowly he released his prisoner and let him sit on the ground, while he kept the .44 tight on him, but not close enough to tempt any attack. He saw now that he needn't have concerned himself with heroics. His prisoner was no hero. He saw too that he was not much more than a boy.

"Why were you watching those two skinners?" Slocum demanded. "Who sent you?"

"You . . . you're Slocum."

"I said, Who sent you!" And he pushed the barrel of the handgun hard into the side of his prisoner's face.

"Jesus!"

"I said whisper! Now tell me!"

"I . . . I dunno . . . I mean . . . I mean Elihu, the reverend, told me . . . I was in the wagon train . . . I saw you . . ."

"Elihu told you. What did he tell you?"

"To foller after Cooch and Emil."

"Why?"

"I dunno."

Slocum jammed the muzzle into the man's face—hard.

"Christ, Slocum . . . take . . . take it slow. I'm telling you—"

"Tell me why he wanted them to be followed."

"He tolt me to listen to them, tell him if they heard anything."

"If *they* heard anything?"

"Yeah. Like maybe they'd talk together about something they heard 'tween you and His Lordship."

Slocum leaned off him a little now, to let him catch his breath. And he wanted a moment to think too.

"So what did you hear?"

"Nothin'. I mean, only bullshit back and forth."

Slocum poked him again with the six-gun. "That's not true. You're lying! Cooch said something about a man telling him something."

"I forgot. Yeah . . . I didn't hear it all . . ."

"Tell me what he said, or you're for the buzzards!"

"I can't—"

"Right now!"

"Something . . . I didn't get it . . . I mean . . ."

Slocum leaned his knee on his prisoner's throat and pushed the six-gun right against his eye.

There was no arguing the Colt .44, and when he released the pressure from his knee the words came.

"Something . . . something like . . . what the man said . . . dunno who the man was."

"What did he say, the man!"

"Said . . . there was dust in them fingernails. That's all. I swear . . . I swear, Slocum. Honest-to-God."

Slocum sat back on his heels. He was listening. All the time of questioning his prisoner he'd been listening. It would have been an easy trap if his quarry had been working with Cooch and Emil and the pair had then bushwhacked him. An old trick. But any trick, old or new, was deadly when it worked.

Still satisfied that there was no trap, that the man was working independently of Emil and Cooch, Slocum stood up. "Get up," he said. And then, "What's your name?"

"Dutch."

"All right, Dutch. You'll ride out of here. You'll get as far away from here as that pony can take you. You understand me?"

"I do."

Slocum had moved closer to the horse now. "I'll take that gun," Slocum said, picking up the six-shooter that had fallen out of its holster. "And this one," he added, slipping the Winchester out of its saddle scabbard. "Put your arms up."

He felt for a belly gun or hideout, and came up with a derringer.

"I see Elihu believes in his men working the advantages." He also saw how Elihu didn't trust anybody.

"You ain't gonna leave me a weapon?"

"You know any other funnies?" He slipped his own six-gun back into its holster. "How old are you, sonny?"

"Should be eighteen if my pa told me right."

"Then you better tell Elihu how lucky you are."

"Lucky?"

"That you're still alive. Now git. And better find yourself a better way of making a living. Stick to cowboying—you look like you've got a feel for horses."

The camp was silent when he returned from his adventure with the kid named Dutch. He had already noted that Lord Frederick and Lady Millecent had separate bedrolls. Maybe just for camping out? He didn't know, and put the thought out of his mind.

He lay now in his own bedroll thinking over all that had happened: with Dutch; with the two skinners, Emil and Cooch; and earlier in the evening with the Edgertons.

They had got the kills they wanted, and the hides were drying. And in the morning they would start back to Little Misery. Yet Slocum had a strong feeling that something was out of line; that he was missing, or not seeing, something. For instance, he had the feeling that the buffalo hunt was actually part of a larger picture, and not something separate in itself. There were just too many connections intertwining with various people for him to think otherwise. People such as Elihu Burlingame, and Monte Kitchen and his friends, for instance. And the two skinners and the young man, Dutch, emphasized the point. Yet still it was vague. So he lay there in his bedroll, letting his mind play with it, not trying to force anything, but simply associating from one thing to another, one event or person to another.

He remembered now how twice the previous evening Lord Frederick had mentioned his uncle, and not just in passing. For instance, he'd wondered aloud where his uncle had been buried. He'd said he had tried to find out in town, but nobody had seemed to know anything. Indeed, it seemed nobody he spoke to had been around when Uncle Harry had visited this country.

Slocum had asked Lord Frederick whether he had checked with the law, and he'd said yes, he had. He'd written them from back home, and had received a reply from the marshal at Mandan that the grave had been unmarked. The reason for this was that the body had only remained there a short while and had then been dug up and shipped back to England.

"I wrote back to the marshal," he'd said, "and asked him where Uncle Harry had actually been buried, but the answer came that nobody seemed to be sure, that the best thing would be for me to come have a look if I were that concerned."

"Well, it was a few years before I got everything together to come out. I mean, time goes on, don't you know. When I got here to Little Muddy, I asked around, but nobody knew anything. None of them were here that long ago, it seems. I hope perhaps I shall find somebody who was, and who might remember something."

"No one recollected anything, eh?" Slocum had asked.

"Oh, a couple or so remembered some English lord coming out and hunting buffalo—I mean, that they'd heard about. Nobody I talked to had actually met Harry."

"Did you go see the marshal on your way out here?" Slocum had then asked.

"Dead. Marshal Lones had succumbed to lead poisoning, to use the terminology of the country," Lord Frederick had said wryly.

"In other words, zero," Slocum had said. "You got nothing."

"Nothing."

The Englishman had tapped his head. "Only this."

"What do you mean?" Slocum asked.

"I don't mean much, actually. But Eddie, Edward, my cousin who was along with Uncle Harry on the hunt, told me where they'd been."

"Well, where did he say? That's all you need to know, isn't it?"

Lord Frederick's bright face had slipped into a wry smile at that point. "Fine. Surely. Etcetera. Simple! Only thing is I was a very young boy at the time, as was Edward, and I don't remember. Only some vague things he told me—like nothing I can even put words to."

"Pictures?" Slocum had asked.

"Something about a huge tower."

"Tower?"

"Yes. Very tall. And they went up it and there were Indian arrowheads there. Here—I've got one." And he reached into his shirt pocket. "I carry it for good luck." And he handed Slocum a small arrowhead.

"Dunno." He felt it carefully. "Looks a little like Arapaho. But it might not be. It's old." He handed it back. "Let me think about it."

"You think you can help me?"

"I don't know. Don't get your hopes up. But you said a tower."

"Eddie called it a huge tower."

"Could be a butte." Then he had asked, "Anybody else know about this? Have you spoken to anybody else?"

"No. No one. I mean, I haven't spoken about the tower."

"I advise you not to."

"But a lot of people know about my looking for my uncle's old grave."

"Is that why you came out here?"

"Yes and no. I had always wanted to come. You know, the Great American West and all that. But then, once decided, I thought I'd see if I could find Uncle Harry's grave; or at any rate, his so-to-say stamping ground."

"Yes," Slocum had said. "I can understand that."

"But why don't you want us to mention this to anyone?" Lady Millecent suddenly asked, after being silent for a long time.

"I was waiting for you to ask me that," Slocum said.

"I wouldn't have slept a minute all night if I hadn't," she responded.

"Because, well, for one thing I know nothing about Uncle Harry, and I get the feeling that neither of you know much about him either. And . . . now this may seem strange to you, and it is only thoughts that have come in since you've been telling me this story, but there may be others interested in Uncle Harry. Have you thought of that?"

"Great Scott, no!" The words burst from Lord Frederick. While his wife said nothing, her mouth formed a round, silent "O."

At the moment Lady Millecent's mouth was again forming a very round "O"—this time on John Slocum's erect penis—as the predawn light began to invade the night sky.

After he had returned from scouting the skinners and his encounter with Dutch, he had lain down on his bedroll, still clothed. Just in case. He slept in the alert way

he always slept on the trail, and when he heard the foot-
steps he came instantly awake.

"Frederick?" he had asked her as she knelt down beside him.

"He's asleep. I hope I'm not disturbing you."

"You are disturbing me. In fact, you've been disturbing me a good while."

Her breath was warm on his lips as she bent down
and pressed her soft, eager mouth to his. She had been
kneeling, and as his arms slid around her she lay down
without any pressure from him, and their bodies fused
in their first embrace.

Already his hand was inside her blouse, cupping her
firm, erect breast, with all the tension in its nipple of
undeniable passion.

"John . . ." She breathed the name into his ear, and
her tongue slipped out to explore, while her hand
slipped into his trousers and circled his member, which
was driving against her. Somehow they got their clothes
off and with both bodies sighing in delight she straddled
his erection and began riding it.

In a moment he had her on her back and had
mounted her, stroking deep and high and slowly into her
wetness, while he smelled the joy of her body heat and
her sex. Undulating in perfect rhythm they let their passion mount—by itself—letting it find its own way, its
own movements and desires en route to the ultimate
ecstasy when they came thrashing in swift, soft, porous
delight which filled them, drained them, and finally sa-
tiated them.

Neither knew or cared how long it had taken. It could
have been a minute or an hour. They lay beside each
other in total joy.

"God, I've been wanting you, John."

"And I've been wanting you. I reckon you knew that."

Her laughter tinkled against the side of his face. "I did. Indeed I did. And every time I knew it my own passion grew for you."

"That's the best way, isn't it?" he said. "To let it grow by itself."

"Oh yes!" And then she said, "But it doesn't hurt to encourage it a little, wouldn't you agree?" And her fingers began to slip along the inside of his thigh.

His organ rose to its supreme length as her touch moved closer to the base of his sex, the root of his now-surging cock, and his balls which she was also fondling.

Grasping the head of his organ, she bent down and rubbed it over her face, into her eyes, along her lips, licking it now with the tip of her tongue, then running her tongue along the great shaft, and finally, just as he was about to go totally crazy, sliding its great thickness into her mouth.

He came enormously, causing her to choke, cough, and for a moment pull away, but then, laughing with joy she gobbled him again, her tongue licking and drawing him until he squirted and kept on squirting, and kept on . . .

After a while he realized the light was coming into the sky. "You'd better get going," he said.

"I will have been for a walk," she said as she pulled on her clothes and stood beside him.

"Come again."

"Oh I will, I will."

The sun was not yet up, but there was more light, heralding its advance from behind the far rimrocks. He rose and walked down to the creek. Stripping, he stepped into the cold water. It was the most wonderful shock, running all the way through his happy body. Coming out of the water, he dried his body with his hands and then pulled on his clothes.

As he walked back to the camp he could smell the delicious aroma of morning coffee. He was ravenously hungry.

6

He was a small, hard man who weighed less than 140 pounds soaking wet; and as those who knew him could attest, he was wont to say that he'd been born too stupid to be scared. His name was Stonebraker.

Slocum spotted him at the bar the moment he walked into the Sure Shot. Stonebraker had spotted him too, he saw; their eyes met in the mirror in back of the bar.

Standing next to the short man, Slocum seemed a towering figure. "Haven't seen you in a spell," he said carefully. "You lookin' for somebody? Not me, leastways, I hope."

Stonebraker's lined face disappeared into a silent guffaw of laughter. "Why no, Slocum. I know you are always damn careful to keep friendly with the law. Course, I ain't kept up with you lately." And the laughter relaxed into a grin.

"I did think I spotted someone in the crowd here a few days back used to work with you—I mean in the old days."

Stonebraker was silent, sipping his beer. Then he

said, lowering his voice, "Let's get over to that there table in the corner. Yonder." And picking up his glass he started off in the direction in which he had nodded. Slocum followed.

It was not Slocum's habit to talk much to lawmen, nor to refer to events that might have taken place in the past—people he had seen, or places he had visited—as he had just done. But he was feeling strangely dry as far as learning anything about Elihu Burlingame and his interest in Lord Frederick. And besides this, he knew for certain that Stonebraker hadn't hit Little Misery because he wanted a rest. The man was here on business; and Stonebraker's business was more often than not hard and dangerous. Slocum had decided not to pussyfoot but to get right into it. And it seemed that Stonebraker felt the same.

"I ain't gonna beat around it, Slocum. You know the name Kyle, do you?"

"Never heard it. He got some summer names maybe?"

"He's the kind of man don't need any," Stonebraker said, and sucked on his teeth for a moment as though looking for a seed to spit out.

They had seated themselves at a round table at the back corner of the room, where they had a full view of the bar, the gaming tables, and most important the swinging doors through which sooner or later the population—at least male—of Little Misery would surely travel.

"Should I?" Slocum said.

"Know the man? No, but you could've heard of him."

"But why ask me?"

"You're a man who gets about."

Slocum took no offense at this. He had known Stonebraker on and off for a long while—Stonebraker and all his aliases.

"You still with the Pinkertons?"

"Let's say I am engaged in a certain research, and my employers put a certain value on what they receive from me, so long as it helps them." He scratched the end of his bony nose. A man in his sixties, Slocum judged, but with the spirit of at least ten, fifteen years less.

"I happen to know a little something about what happened up there at Medicine Gap," Stonebraker said. And he lowered one eyelid slowly, while keeping his other eye wide open. "If you catch my drift."

Slocum caught his drift real fast. A little business with unbranded slicks, and the other side of the law had taken the stiff attitude of worrying him about it. He could have stayed in Medicine Gap and worked it through—the misunderstanding—but it would have taken time, and then there was always the risk of something else, say from the past, getting uncovered. It was best to leave. Which he had done. And pronto.

And right then, as if to emphasize his point, Stonebraker reached into the pocket of his loose-fitting coat and pulled out a dodger. "You seen this?"

"Is there a picture?"

"Just a description."

"It could be somebody else."

"It isn't somebody else."

Slocum took a swallow from his glass. He knew he could have gotten out of it. He could outdraw Stonebraker, he knew, though the man was fast. Or he could leave town. But it wasn't all that bad. It just *looked* bad, helping some of the nesters get their stock back. Hell, branding slicks was a common practice. Fact was, the big ranchers all did it. Always had. But the stock growers and the association had to have it their way. And anyway, he liked Stonebraker; it wouldn't do to throw down on such a man. At the same time, he sure didn't want to be euchred into something—which he could see coming.

"Tell me what you want," he said. "But tell me easy."

"Just want you to maybe notice here and there."

Slocum looked down at the dodger that the law at Medicine Gap or the association had somehow gotten out on him, or likely both. Lucky there was no picture. But they had the name.

"It looks like a fake to me," he said.

"That it is." Stonebraker took a pull at his beer, licked the foam from his lips, and wiped his gray mustache with the back of his hand. He was a man with a very bony face, but the mustache did him justice. Slocum had long ago decided that when you first looked at Stonebraker he looked like a nice old man, but when you looked again you could see he was nobody to mess with. It paid then to take a second look at things. Which Slocum, being part Indian, always did.

"So you want me to keep an ear to the ground, and let you know if I come up with anything."

"That's the size of it."

"And we can forget about this then." And Slocum tapped the folded dodger with his forefinger.

"The association still has them going about, but not too far. I'll dampen it. Though—depends," he added, sly.

"Why are they being so careful? Afraid somebody might follow it up and get too close to themselves, are they?"

"You said it." A grin appeared suddenly on Stone-braker's craggy face.

They were silent for some moments then, drinking their beer, each with his own thoughts.

"Tell me about this fellow Kyle," Slocum said.

"He's an operator. He pulls swindles that are pretty hard to spot. You've heard of the diamond mine in Nevada? He salted the whole thing. Got clean away with it, and nobody can prove nothing. Took some bankers in San Francisco and New York. Took 'em right to the shearing shed. Got off free as air."

"And you're saying he's into something here."

Stonebraker sniffed. "What I am saying is he'll be too smart to pull anything like that again for a while. See, everybody knew he did it, but nobody could prove anything." He took out a cigar and bit off the little bullet at the end and spat it out. "I know there's an old abandoned mine at Mud Creek, not far from here. You know anything about it?"

"I've heard of it. And I've also heard of the Lost Coker Mine; but nobody knows anything worth listening to, though I understand a lot of pilgrims have tried to find the Lost Coker."

Stonebraker had lighted his cigar. "You know anything about this feller from England and his wife; this Lord Frederick Edgerton?"

Slocum told him what he knew, relating the details of the buffalo hunt, but withholding information on the two skinners, and most decidedly on the sexual prowess of Lady Millecent.

He felt a strong prompting not to tell everything to the lawman right away. There was always a moment when you needed something extra—often in the form of information that was useful—and he wanted to hold what he could in reserve until he understood more what it meant. Thus he related only the obvious details about Lord Frederick and his charming wife. After all, he also knew that Stonebraker was a dedicated lawman.

They finished their beer and shortly left the Sure Shot—separately. Slocum realized full well that Harelip Schneider behind the bar, as well as the Sure Shot's owner, Packy O'Gatty, and some more of the clientele were fully aware of the presence of John Slocum conversing with the new man in town. It would only be a matter of time before someone came up with who that stranger really was. But all to the good, it might flush something, or even someone.

As he walked away from the Sure Shot, Slocum remembered how he had mentioned to Stonebraker having maybe seen an old colleague of his a few days before in the saloon. But there had been no response from the lawman.

One of Horatio Kyle's favorite pastimes was browsing through the newspapers, especially those published in the western territories. As far as he was concerned, nothing in the East—or anywhere, for that matter—could beat those frontier organs for flair, entertainment, and outstanding humor. Furthermore, they were indeed rich with useful information.

Kyle especially enjoyed reading about his own exploits. Sometimes his name appeared in some aspect of a story, and depending upon how much his coattails were clear of any scandal, suspicious behavior, or lawless conduct, he richly enjoyed the report. Usually the writer had the story wrong, but then, of course, only an insider—really only himself—was in a position to know the truth.

Thus, he had enjoyed greatly reading about the Great Desert Diamond Hoax. It had been a high point in his career; it had resulted in a fantastic return on his investment; and best of all, he had duped some of the smartest financial minds in the country, especially in California and New York, plus a couple more in London.

An abandoned child, Horatio had been raised by an extraordinary gentleman whose pleasure in life was immense; a man who loved wine, women, and song, living his life to the hilt. Moreover, a man who was a master at his chosen profession. Holy John Swayles could stack a deck of cards quicker than a man could scratch his own behind, and do it right in front of your eyes. So it was said; and Kyle, his adopted disciple, knew it to be so.

The story went, as Holy John told it, that the boy had been left in a Kansas City whorehouse when his mother had to take it on the lam and leave town with all possible speed. Obviously having a small child along would simply have slowed any sort of fast travel.

Holy John, being a literary man as well as a full-time gambler on the Mississippi, and later on the trains that were traversing the continent, had named the boy Horatio after Horatio Nelson, the hero of Trafalgar. The name Kyle had come from a tobacco can the boy had with him at the time Holy John found him, and in which he carried his worldly possessions—dice, a top, some string, and a bent pin for fishing.

Holy John Swayles taught the boy everything he knew, plus a lot of things he didn't. His pupil proved to be all that he could have wanted. He learned quickly, and very early on showed an ability to improvise, which was the main principle of his master's teaching. Horatio understood fully not only the craft of his mentor's profession, but its art. He was pleased that Holy John died proud of his disciple.

Times were different now than in the great days of the riverboats. For a while Kyle had worked the railroads. But at one point a particular operation, involving real estate sold on the belief that the property on which the house stood was actually a silver mine, drew him to another facet of his career. Cards, dice, horses were all very well, but the big excitement—not to mention profit—lay in duping the rich fools who seemed so numerous, especially in the new West. People looking for profit, their greed drooling from their mouths and fingers, were a dime a dozen, as the saying had it. And if he, Kyle, didn't take their money, somebody else would. For he had discovered that amazing facet of the human being: That he will dupe himself willingly, happily; he will beg you to take his money. Holy John had told him that over and over, but it was the actual discovery by himself that fascinated Horatio Kyle and set him firmly and happily on his career. For he understood wholly the remark that Holy John had been drilling into him that the greener, the dude will find you. "It is because," Holy John had told him in one of his innumerable lectures on "The Art of the Game," "it is because well nigh each and every member of our great community of man is all but consumed with the desire that burns in him to get something for nothing. Show one of these saps a way to cheat the other saps in the world and he will do anything you want, my boy, I say anything!"

It was true. Look at the salted diamond mine! He— Horatio Kyle—had cleaned up. And when the caper was discovered as a con, the law couldn't lay a finger on him. The saps had *forced* money on him, begged him to let him take them, or to show them, rather, how to cheat themselves through their own dishonesty. Beautiful!

At the moment as he sat in the front room of the Inter-Ocean Hotel in Cheyenne, he had just completed the final stages of his plan for his latest game. Kyle liked the word "game." Life was a game, and he saw himself as a gamesman. This game, though, was going to outdo even the Diamond Mine Hoax, as the newspapers had so brilliantly called it.

Once more he went over his latest aspect of the plan, which his "dynamiters," as he called them, were busily executing up in Little Muddy. And he was going to clean up even better than he'd managed with the diamond game, when he'd had to spend a load on gem experts, miners, geologists, and other, more mundane, but also necessary persons who carried out the actual work.

Now, going over the personnel of his present game, he drew satisfaction that he had selected, after much trouble, a good crew. Chuck Delaney had always pulled his oar, though he was now and again uppity. He would have to watch Delaney, keep an eye on him. He was getting just a bit high in the pockets. Myrtle was trustworthy, he could swear to that; and the kid, well, she would handle the kid.

He grinned. He should have run a theater, what with all the aliases. Like that geologist in the diamond thing, and those prospectors—hardly knew a pick from a shovel! But Delaney, now, was a reverend type, all right. Delaney liked to really be his part, whatever it was—a reverend, a schoolteacher, a retired Army officer. In the diamond scam he'd played a prospector.

He chuckled, remembering the times Holy John had him pretend all kinds of things to lure the saps—a schoolboy on vacation from a rich eastern school, an English kid whose parents had died tragically in a disaster at sea, a poor downtrodden orphan whose mother had been raped and burned alive by Indians. It had all been fun, and also rewarding.

Suddenly a thought swept into his head and he sat up in his chair, almost as though galvanized. God, why hadn't he thought of that before!

But the great thought was interrupted by the opening of the door that connected the room he was in with the hotel lobby. He turned with irritation, for he'd wanted the room to himself—it was a quiet, private place with newspapers on a big table and comfortable armchairs. But his irritation vanished when he saw who it was.

"How are you, darling?" the young woman asked. "Would you care for a cup of coffee?"

"My dear, with you even a cup of arsenic would taste marvelous."

"My, how gallant!" And her laughter tinkled like silver in the room as Kyle swept to his feet, bounced forward, and, taking her hand, bent to kiss it.

"Only my hand?"

"Later, my dear." He stood right before her, feasting his eyes. She was young, maybe thirty, with a full figure in freshly washed gingham. Her eyes sparkled. Her dark hair swept up above her ears, which he found delightful.

"Always a new way of doing your hair," he said.

"I've taken the liberty of already ordering coffee, so be careful, Mr. Kyle, the man will be here in a moment."

Kyle tore his eyes away from her and strode to the full-length mirror that stood near a corner of the room. Why it was in the room at all, which was actually more of a smoking room then anything else, he didn't know. But he found it useful, for he was a man who took pains with his appearance. In fact, one of the reasons he liked Amelia so much was that she was the same way about herself.

He stood looking at himself, adjusting his cravat. He saw an average-height man of forty, with thick shoulders; and yes, a horsey face, but one that showed character, with a strong nose and jaw, a firm, determined mouth, and dark blue eyes under a high forehead. The eyes were widely spaced, which he liked, and the brows were just the right thickness; he trimmed them every other day or so. Yes, he liked what he was seeing. He always did, for that matter.

"My dear, you look beautiful."

"Handsome!" he corrected. "Women are beautiful, though not all by a long shot. Not nearly as beautiful as you, my darling. And as for me—yes, handsome. But" —and he turned to catch a side look at himself—"there are not many like what I see. You can take it from me. Modest as I am, I am compelled to admit that I have not only educated myself from below zero all the way up to the top, but my rugged and at the same time refined looks have equaled my, shall we say, not exalted, but reasonably high station in life. Eh?" He turned to her, cocking a racy eye as he regarded her full bosom.

There was a knock on the door, and a waiter came with the coffee.

"I've just had a brilliant idea," Kyle said, when the man had left, closing the door softly behind him. "But it will have to wait. I'll tell you later. Meanwhile, I want to have our coffee in peace and quiet—hoping we are not interrupted—and then we..." He paused, his eyes feeding on her lovely face, her body, admiring very much the angle of her wrist as she lifted her cup.

She was watching him, a suggestion of a smile at the corners of her full lips. "And then we . . . what?"

"Well . . ." He cleared his throat, though it didn't need it. "I've a luncheon appointment at the Cheyenne Club with some business associates, or I should say, possible business associates. But, er, we might have a moment or so."

"We, er, might." And she sipped her coffee.

"I thought that since I have sort of, well, taken on your education in certain areas, my dear, that we might continue where we left off earlier in the day."

"The geography lesson?"

"We could. But the anatomy lesson might be more rewarding."

"I suggest whatever you suggest," she said easily. She laughed, and he instantly joined her.

"It makes a helluva lot of diff, doesn't it, Horatio, my dear; a helluva lot of diff what we choose to play at—since it always ends up in bed."

He had risen, and now with his erection making a tent out of his trousers he came toward her.

Taking her head in his two hands he bent toward her while her hand came up and squeezed his penis.

"I think it's bedtime," Kyle said.

"If we don't get up there damn fast," she said, "I'm going to have you right on the floor, and I don't give a hoot who comes in!"

And again they had a good laugh. Going through the lobby and up the stairs, they could hardly restrain themselves from bursting into further laughter.

In another moment they were in his room.

"I must not forget the time," he said. "I have my appointment at the Cheyenne Club."

"Horatio—fuck the Cheyenne Club."

Horatio was fully equal to the moment—as usual. "No, my dear. Fuck you!"

"You'd better show me what you mean by that smart remark, mister."

And Horatio Kyle, having been raised by the great Holy John Swayles to be, if not a full-scale gentleman, then at least an industrious contributor to the sexual health of the opposite sex, and at the most an assiduous burnisher of his own fascinating self-portrait, showed her.

All at once he was wide awake. He lay on his bedroll with his hand holding the .44, relaxing himself so that he could allow the sounds to come into him. It was an old trick he had learned from a Paiute—not to try hearing "like a white man," tensing himself, and going out to listen, but to relax and soften the body so that the sound could come into him.

Overhead the moon had just risen, and he could see the tops of the trees clearly against the lighted darkness of the deep sky. He heard the Appaloosa moving nearby, and the coughing bark of a coyote farther away.

After talking with Stonebraker he had decided to get out of town for a day or two. He wanted to think it all out—the buffalo hunt and its hunters, the wagon train with Elihu Burlingame, the fight with The Allen, the sudden presence of Stonebraker on the scene, and for sure his encounter with the boy named Dutch.

Something damned funny was going on with the Edgertons in the middle of it. There was also Lord Frederick's searching for his uncle's temporary grave. Why? Was it truly sentiment on his part? Or was there something more to it?

No, he did feel that Lord Frederick's feeling for his

uncle was sincere; that he did indeed want to see the West where Uncle Harry had been, and about which he had written about so happily. And surely, too, it was legitimate that he and Lady Millecent wanted to shoot a buffalo or two. They were rich, they were young, they wanted to have fun. The West had known a lot of visiting nobles like them.

But—and this was the point—someone else was interested in their activities. It was a feeling he had more than anything else. Someone, or maybe a few people, were interested in the Edgertons just a little more than seemed necessary.

For instance, the speed, the ease, and the enthusiasm to get Lord Frederick out on the hunt. And Elihu offering himself, Slocum, as a guide. And that fellow Monte Kitchen and the plan that everyone was talking about now of the slaughterhouse to be built in Little Misery with Edgerton and his crew headed by Kitchen sending dressed beef direct to Chicago.

Slocum had pointed out that the plan wouldn't work, any more than Lord Frederick's great buffalo hunt had been more than a whimper; for as he told Frederick and Millecent and anyone else who wanted to hear—and it was what any cattleman could have said—the eastern dealers would never buy steers fed on grass alone, for the public wanted meat from animals corn-fattened in the stockyards before slaughtering.

Lord Frederick had refused to admit this crushing oversight, but his wife had listened to Slocum, and he hoped that she would have her way. He thought she would.

The point was that all of this revealed a situation where it was becoming more and more obvious that Lord Frederick Edgerton was being set up, bilked, suckered like any greenhorn or tenderfoot with "nary a corn and nary a callus."

Meanwhile, Stonebraker. Slocum knew him as one of the shrewdest, toughest lawmen he'd ever encountered—and he had encountered a goodly number. Stonebraker was not here wasting his time. Nor was he here on his own. Formerly, he had been a Pinkerton, but he could be a range detective now for the association, or it could be Wells, Fargo, or even the U.S. government maybe. It didn't matter so much who his employer was. What mattered was that somebody thought the present action in Little Misery worthy of first-class attention.

Stonebraker, Slocum knew, had one alarming specialty: He was totally disarming. Thus he had always been an ace at winning people's confidence, at disguising himself in some role that no one would dream of suspecting. He had been known to worm his way into the confidence of the most dangerous and intelligent conmen. The hard fact was that notorious criminals trusted him—until they discovered too late who he in fact was.

And now he suddenly remembered Olive. It was Olive he had seen in the crowd at the Sure Shot. Olive! And it was no wonder Stonebraker had ignored his question. Stonebraker had been known to work with Olive. Olive was a half-breed, an ace tracker, a mountain man, a rough-and-tumble boy, and a crack shot. He was a killer. And Slocum knew he had worked with Stonebraker—though in just what capacity he wasn't sure. He had a notion that the detective used Olive as a menace, a threat, as backup maybe, but in actual fact did all the dirty work himself, made his own arrests after finding his own evidence. But Slocum understood full well the advantage psychologically of having a man like Olive at hand. The threat, in some cases, when used well, as he knew a man such as Stonebraker would indeed use it, could be much more effective than actual physical action. Thinking about it now, he remembered things he had heard about Stonebraker, and this particular characteristic of the man—to move quietly and swiftly but to carry a stick of dynamite as a threat—and how much more effective that was, that threat, than the actual gunning. His respect for the little lawman had always been high, but now it rose even higher.

He continued to lie there on his bedroll while his thoughts moved through all the material that now for the first time seemed to be falling into some kind of order.

Suddenly he sat right up on his bedroll. "Dust," the man had said. At least that was what Dutch had told him Cooch had said. "Dust in those fingernails."

And now everything cleared and he saw at once what was happening. There was only one kind of dust that would excite such comment. One and only one.

Slocum was already on his feet and rolling his bedroll. The predawn light was just coming into the sky as he rode out, heading back for Little Misery. He knew now exactly what he was looking for. And he knew what somebody else was certainly looking for.

7

Meanwhile, plans went ahead for building the abattoir, or as Three-Card Monte Kitchen and the boys put it, the "bat house." In the process they were relieving Lord Frederick of the tidy sum of $100,000. The abattoir actually cost half that, but there were hungry mouths and starving hands to be cared for. And His Lordship didn't seem to object. Indeed, he was happy, and was now planning to build a mansion for himself and his love— or, as he called it, a château, modeled more or less inexactly upon various châteaux he had visited in France.

The boys were delighted at the prospect.

"It's going to cost him a packet," Bill Forefinger predicted.

"More'n the bat house, I'd wager," Packy O'Gatty said, his voice almost singing with delight at the prospect.

They were seated around their customary table at the Sure Shot—Three-Card, Bill Forefinger, O'Gatty, Cy

Pone, Clem Abernathy, but without Elbows McFadden, who was down with the croup.

"I'm concerned about this man Slocum," Three-Card was saying, as Harelip Schneider, the current bartender, brought in more refreshment. "You seen him about, Harelip?"

"Nary hair nor hide," Harelip swiftly retorted. Then he paused, his dim eyes studying the atmosphere immediately in front of him.

"You got something?" Packy O'Gatty said.

"Naw. Only was thinking about that feller, the stringy little bugger what was here one time, and I ain't seen him neither."

"Hunh." The grunt came from Cy Pone, a man with protruding eyes that were like knobs, giving him the expression of someone perpetually astonished. Cy ran the Doggone Eatery, and his deceased father-in-law had met Harry Edgerton many years ago when the Englishman had come west and shot buffalo, elk, deer, antelope, and God knows what else and had ended up "massacred by the Arapahoes." "He put me in mind of a lawman," Cy now said, and he popped another plug of tobacco into his mouth, having just sliced it off his supply with his pocketknife.

"What makes you say that, Cy?" Abernathy said, scratching his bald head.

"Just feel it. He has got that look, that smell."

"I took him for a prospector," O'Gatty said.

Harelip was moving toward the door, saying, "I better get back to the bar."

"You got a line on him, Harelip?" O'Gatty asked. "The stranger."

"I took him for a prospector too. For the matter of

that he did ask about the old Coker Mine." Harelip had paused with his hand on the door.

"What did you tell him?"

"Told him nobody knew where it was. Said it'd been lost since . . . hell, way back in the Indian Wars."

"Since Christ was a corporal," said Clem Abernathy in a heavy voice as Harelip left the room.

"You hear anything about Slocum, Clem?" Three-Card asked. "He was staying at your place, wasn't he?"

"He took off a couple days ago, left some gear with the desk clerk, Johnnie, saying he'd be back, but wasn't sure just when." He paused to take a drink. "Did you want to know what was in his warbag?"

"We was just waitin' on you tellin' us," Cy Pone said, his voice wry.

Clem took another pull at his glass. "Nothing very much!" He coughed out a laugh. "Exceptin' a dodger, by golly! It appears Mr. Slocum is wanted by the Stock-grower's Association up in Buffalo County."

Somebody emitted a low whistle.

Three-Card said, "Then it looks like that stringy little gent ain't a lawman."

Packy O'Gatty nodded. "Else he'd be takin' the man in."

"So maybe he is looking for the Coker, after all," Bill Forefinger said. "What the hell, everybody's been lookin' for it, or dreamin' about it, ever since way back whenever it was it got lost."

"Well, as we all know, the ground's been covered from here all the way to hell an' breakfast," Three-Card Monte said.

"And back," added Cy Pone.

"Used to be people figured it could of been connected to the Mud River vein up at Pine Hill." Abernathy looked down at the backs of his hands, which were lying on top of the round table. "People were certain, and I remember, they swore it had to be up that way."

"Connected, you're sayin'?" Cy leaned forward with his fat elbows on the table.

"That's what everybody used to be figurin' until they gave up on it. But my theory is it ain't anywheres near the Mud River."

"The Coker?"

"The Lost Coker. I doubt it ever existed excepting in some liquored-up old sourdough's dreaming."

"Let's get back to Slocum," Three-Card said, lowering his glass and placing it carefully in front of him.

"Well, what about him?" Cy asked, canting his head at Three-Card. "You look like you got something up your sleeve, Three-Card."

"Mister, don't never say that to a gambling man."

And this brought a roar of delight from the table.

Three-Card looked down at his hands, which were loosely circling his glass of whiskey. "Slocum busted the shit out of that feller I got from the wagon train to keep an eye on Cooch and Emil."

"What I don't understand, Monte, is why you set that up. Why did you want to foller those two miserable skinners in the first place?" Abernathy asked.

"On account of I don't trust 'em. And neither does Burlingame."

"Then why did you offer them to work for His Lordship? I figgered you had a reason for it, like wanting to know what went on—especially with Slocum there. But why? Why does His Lordship's buff hunting interest us?" It was Bill Forefinger speaking, and when he finished he ran his hand across his mouth as though wiping it dry.

"You can't always get the men you want," Monte Kitchen explained. "Those two boys were the only skinners around, since there ain't hardly a buffalo between here and the North Pole. And since I couldn't trust 'em, I sicced the kid onto them, figurin' with a pair such as them two if there was anything come up about anything then they might decide to keep it to theirselves. You follow me?"

"I follow you," Abernathy said. "And when you speak about 'anything' that might come up during the hunt for the buffs, you are of course talking about . . ." And he let it hang, his thick eyebrows rising into his forehead, while his eyes held Three-Card in the question.

"The Lost Coker," interjected Bill Forefinger at that point. "What else?" he asked the table. "What else could it be?"

Three-Card grinned at his colleagues. "We remember, do we not, the fact that His Lordship's uncle was out here and got shot up by Injuns. See, I have been wondering how much Lord Frederick came out here to see the country and hunt buffs and how much he came out trying to locate something about his Uncle Henry."

"Harry," Cy Pone swiftly corrected.

Three-Card threw his hands suddenly at the ceiling of the smoke-filled room. "Harry, Henry, Horace—who the hell cares! It was him, the uncle, I am sayin', being the reason he come all the way out here from England."

"What the hell are we all talking about, for Christ sake?" demanded Packy O'Gatty. "That was a helluva while back, the uncle's visit. A helluva while. Nobody's even around who remembers the man. So what are we talking about?"

"What are we talking about?" Three-Card turned his full attention onto the proprietor of the Sure Shot. And then in a softer voice, a voice loaded with patience, he addressed the ceiling. "We are talking about gold." He lowered his eyes to look directly at Mr. O'Gatty. "We are talking about the Lost Coker Mine, my friend."

Almost, though not precisely, at the same moment that Three-Card Monte Kitchen said those electrifying words, John Slocum was at Drover, nearly 200 miles away, addressing Mr. Arnot Amunsen on a closely related subject. This was the exhumation of the body of Lord Harold Edgerton from where it had been buried after the Indian fight a number of years earlier, and the shipment of his remains to the Edgerton home in Dorset, England.

Arnot Amunsen had been the town undertaker at the time, and had officiated at the removal of the body from its grave and the shipment of same. A man of one hundred winters and ninety-nine summers, the retired undertaker expected soon to be one hundred and one. Erect, vigorous, though forgetful, with one glass eye, and skin that looked to be tough as dried buffalo hide, Amunsen answered Slocum's questions with an expression of amusement in his watery blue eyes.

"I feel that you've been questioned before on this matter," Slocum said. "I don't believe I am the first."

"That is the truth." The man's voice was firm with what he considered the gravity of the situation, not to mention its unique qualifications for brisk gossip.

"Would you tell me the name of the person who

asked about this? Was it Lord Frederick Edgerton, or perhaps his wife?" Slocum asked.

"Lord . . . who?"

"I reckon it wasn't him."

"A man name of Snapes come to see me, a good while back, like 'fore Christmas."

"Snapes? Was that his real name?"

"How the hell would I know? Is Slocum your real name?"

Slocum broke out laughing at that. The old man was a feisty rooster. Well, he had asked for it. But he had wanted to see how much sand that rooster had in his craw.

"What did he want to know?"

"About the corpse—the twenty-year-old corpse by now, I reckon."

"Could you tell me what the man looked like?"

"I see you don't believe the feller was using his real name."

"I know *I* wouldn't, if it was me."

The old man snorted, and spat—plumb center into the cuspidor.

"What did he ask about?"

"I don't remember much—but like how long had he been buried at the place where he got shot. Was the body in good condition. All stuff like that. Nothing important. Hell, I found out he was some English lord type, somebody rich and important. But he sure didn't look so important lying there in that shallow grave. And he was real deader'n hell."

"Were there any possessions with him? Money? Letters?"

"Only some papers—letters actually—giving his name and where he come from. Nothing important.

Hell, I just packed him down to Drover here and got Jiminy Johannsen to build him a box, and then when his brother showed up right then we shipped him back home."

"But did you notice anything fishy about the thing?"

"Fishy? Hell, man, you ask the same questions like that newspaper feller ast."

"Newspaper man?"

"Snapes! Snapes, that feller."

"What about any gold on him?" Slocum asked, finally coming to the main purpose of his visit.

But the old man was shaking his head. "Didn't see any gold on him. Hell, I would've noticed that first off!"

"Like in his fingernails. Gold dust?"

"I examined the corpse from head to toe—all the hell over and everywheres. Just like any other corpse that got buried with lead in his body."

"Did you notice his fingernails, though? I mean, were they long, short? Did they look as though they might have been cut recently?"

The former undertaker was shaking his head, his mouth forming a silent no. "No sir! No one had tampered with the corpse, I mean that anybody could tell. I want you to know that I know my business, mister, and when I say something about a corpse, I know what I am talking about."

"I've got one last question, Mr. Amunsen."

"Shoot, young feller. I got to take a leak, and I bin waitin' for you to get to the end of what you wanted to say."

"Was the corpse, the body, the body of Lord Harold Edgerton?"

"It was identified by his brother, who come over special for to do it."

"Thank you, Mr. Amunsen."

But Arnot Amunsen had sped to the door to relieve himself, and very likely hadn't heard.

He had spent two days trying to locate the towers or buttes that Lord Frederick had described, but though there were the twin buttes at Blue Crossing, there didn't appear to be anything that would have meant gold. He spent most of one day checking along the crossing and also at Willow Creek, where Harry was supposed to have been killed by the Indians.

Yet the visit with Arnot Amunsen in Drover encouraged him. Meeting with Stonebraker one night in the Stud he gave him his news.

"Good to see you're right on it, Slocum," Stonebraker said. "I heard you had yourself a handful or two with The Allen here." He had lowered his voice as they both saw the owner of the Stud enter the premises.

"Here he comes," Stonebraker said, without looking up.

Slocum had already spotted the move toward him, and was ready as the booming voice hit all the way through the big tent.

"Slocum!"

Slocum leaned back in his chair carefully, but with his balance and his two feet placed so that he could move on the instant. "That's my name, mister."

Slocum had his eyes on the big man's ugly face, but he was also seeing his huge hands, which he was holding loosely together at his waist. By keeping his eyes relaxed, Slocum was able to increase his vision, that is, he could widen it by not staring hard at anything. It was a trick he had learned—along with much else—from the Indians.

"Tomorrow is the Fourth of July, and I'm challenging you to fight me for the champeenship of Wyoming, in fact, the whole of the western country, by God. And you better get your ass ready in that ring when the boys pitch it. In fact, I believe we'll fight for the champeenship of the whole of America. I was champ once, by God, and when I whip your yellow ass I will be again!"

Almost before these words were out of his mouth Slocum was out of his chair and had kicked The in the kneecap, bringing forth a scream of pain and curses, and had then brought down a vicious right hook right behind the man's ear as he bent in agony. It was exactly the spot where he had hit him in their previous fight. And again The Allen fell like a log to the ground. He was all but out, as he lay on the dirt, emitting wet grunts and hollow curses while fighting to stay conscious.

"Jesus," said Stonebraker.

"Jesus had nothing to do with it," Slocum said.

"I got to remember never to challenge you for the heavyweight championship of America, by jingo."

"Not if you're carrying a lead pipe in your rear pocket like that sonofabitch was," Slocum said, bending down and pulling out the wicked weapon and tossing it onto the ground well away from The.

"You're sharp, Slocum," said Stonebraker bringing a plug of tobacco out of his shirt pocket. "It's why I be glad to have you workin' with me." He pulled out a knife and began cutting himself a slice of tobacco. "How'd you know he had that thing in his pocket?"

"I didn't know. I just knew he had something when I saw him shift his weight and his right hand twitched." He moved out of the way as two men came to help The to his feet. "You know just as well as me that a bugger like himself there isn't going to offer you a fair fight like that unless he's fixing to get your guard down."

The Allen was on his feet now, but unsteady as he faced the man who had knocked him out for the second time running.

"You been lucky, Slocum, but I'll get you. I promise you that. I'll get you!"

"Then I'll be expecting you, The," Slocum said, and taking out a quirly he lighted it, striking the wooden lucifer along the underside of his thigh as he lifted his leg.

"Let *us* take care of him, boss," said one of the men who had helped the giant to his feet.

"Naw! I'll get the sonofabitch myself. He's been lucky twicet now. But next time . . ." He let the sentence hang as he turned and removed himself from the scene.

Shortly, the Stud returned to its normal tempo, while a lot of eyes followed John Slocum as he and Stonebraker took their departure.

In the street Slocum said, "I've been looking into some things, and when they click into place I'll be talking to you."

"Good enough. Meanwhile we better keep apart."

Slocum nodded. "I was figuring the same."

"Watch your back trail, Slocum."

"I figured you were watching it, Stonebraker," Slocum said, with a curt nod and a little laugh inside at how he'd cut the lawman to size, as he headed down the street.

It had been a good long while since Slocum had seen Nellie, except twice briefly from across the street, and he was pleased when he ran into her outside the Hotel de Paris.

"Hi, Slocum. I saw you in the Stud, and I wanted to fix it so I bumped into you without it being too noticeable." Her smile was not only in her face but all through her, he could tell. Her eyes were dancing, and he knew his own were too.

He didn't say anything more until they were up in his room.

"Of course, being here in Abernathy's place is like being out in the middle of the street as far as minding your own business," she said.

"Do you care?" he asked, turning toward her after he'd locked the door.

"No. But I'm worried about you, Slocum. The is going to get you in the back."

"I don't think so."

"Don't be foolish." She had sat down on the edge of the bed with her hands in her lap and was looking at him, a beseeching look in her face.

"Right now I haven't got time to think whether I'm being foolish or not," he said.

"He won't rest till he gets you. You've put him down twice now. Twice! Slocum, you're crazy!"

"Crazy about you, I am for sure," he said, standing right in front of her. "Look, don't worry. The wants to beat me fair and square—more or less."

"How do you know that?"

"He's the type who wouldn't want anyone to think he took unfair advantage in beating someone. He's not a back-shooter—at least in this case. Maybe with others, but not now. His pride is more important to him than simply killing me. It's important how he would kill me. He wants to do it with his fists."

"Slocum, you're crazy if you believe that."

"I don't believe it."

"What the hell are you saying!" Her mouth fell open in astonishment.

"I'm telling you how he figures things, see. But I'm also aware of the fact that something might make him decide to act differently. He did have that lead pipe in his pocket. See, the thing is to figure a man out, right? And then you got to figure out how he wouldn't act, and you treat him like that. Both ways. Like he was two and not just one. That way you're not surprised. But shut up now will you, damn it!"

She had laid her face against his bulging trousers, and reaching behind him held his buttocks, pulling him to her.

Slocum's fingers, meanwhile, were unbuttoning her dress. It seemed endless before he had gotten the buttons and hooks undone and had his hand on her cool, quivering breast with its nipple as hard as a finger. Then as he remained standing and while she unbuttoned his pants he slipped her dress down and found her other breast.

She had his cock out now and was holding its head on her right nipple, then began to circle it around, then she held her nipple in the wet hole at the end of his organ.

Her mouth was as soft and ripe as a perfect peach when she slid it around his enormous shaft. Slowly she began to suck, meanwhile pulling down his trousers, pulling down his drawers, taking his balls in one hand,

and running her fingers down the crack between his buttocks with the other.

They were on the bed now, naked, and he mounted
her from the side, while she brought her leg up onto his
shoulder. Then he shifted her onto her back and she had
both legs on his shoulders, while he pulled her buttocks
up onto his thrusting penis as their juices mingled into
delightful little noises and they pumped in unison.

Now she brought her legs down, and without separating he was on his back and she was sitting on him with
her back to him and with his swollen member riding
deep into her from the rear.

"Oh, come!" she whispered. "Come . . . my God,
give it to me!"

Her buttocks rose and lowered and then squirmed on
his great stick as they rutted with the abandon of the
most delightful and elemental barnyard necessity—until
they both came, splashing each other with their exqui-
sitely tuned passion in an explosion that brought them
gasping into collapse next to each other, with arms and
legs entwined, though neither knew how they'd ever
gotten into such a position.

They rested.

After what seemed a long time she said, "Boy, you
are the best ever, Slocum."

"I know," he said, laying on the modesty to make her
laugh. "But you bring out the best in me, young lady."

"I want you to live long enough to do it with me
often."

"Let's not get into that again."

"Sorry. But I like you."

"Prove it."

"Slocum, I know you don't like me to pick at you,

and I won't. I'll only say it just this one more time.
Please, please be careful. I work with The and his boys.
I know that sonofabitch who came in with the Conestogas, too. I see you talking to him sometimes. I
wouldn't trust that man in a church, let alone in a saloon
or on the street."

"What do you know about a man named Three-Card
Monte?"

"I don't know him. He comes in for a push with one
of my girls every now and again. He's a slicker, that's
for sure. Always trying to get it for free, Millie tells
me."

"Ever hear of someone named Kyle?"

"No. Man or woman?"

"Man, I guess."

"You don't know him?"

"Uh-uh."

"Kyle. I'll keep an ear out. Anyone else?"

"You know anything about this lost gold mine, the
Coker?"

"I know it's sort of mentioned here and there, but I
don't believe anybody knows where the hell it is. Why,
are you looking for it?"

His hand had dropped down on her thigh and now
moved up to fondle her damp bush. "This here is my
gold mine," he said.

"You feel like doing a little mining?"

"Would you join me?"

"Do you have to ask?" she whispered as she rolled
over on top of him, with her thighs straddling his hips as
she rode down onto his erection.

This time they came together with Nellie on top, as
she collapsed onto him quivering with total ecstasy as

he drove into her as deep and as high as he could get, flooding her with his come, while he thought of nothing, remembered nothing, only knew this moment of total astonishment.

After a few minutes she spoke. "Slocum . . ."

"I will take care of myself."

"That isn't what I was going to say."

"What then?"

"I want to do it again."

"So do I." He put his hand on her belly button. "Except you don't," he said.

"What the hell do you know!"

"If you really wanted to do it again you'd do it, you wouldn't talk about it."

She was silent, and suddenly he felt her tears on his shoulder.

"I'm sorry, Slocum. What you say is true. I meant, I want to see you again. Do it again maybe later, or tomorrow, or soon. Like that."

"I know what you meant," he said, and his voice was gentle as he reached over and touched the side of her face. She was still crying.

"I'm ashamed."

"Stop talking like that. Didn't I already tell you it's good to cry."

"Well, damn it, I'm following your instructions, aren't I?"

"Why don't you sleep?"

"I don't want to sleep."

"So don't." He sat up, feeling something had changed in the atmosphere of the room.

"Slocum . . ."

"Yeah." He was sitting up on the edge of the bed,

with his feet on the floor. He turned his head to look down at her.

"I lied to you."

"About Kyle."

"How did you guess?"

"That's the only important thing that you could have lied about. That's how."

8

When Harelip Schneider walked into the back room at the Sure Shot with coffee for the boys he announced that the forty-year-old widow Practice Calisher had given birth to twin boys.

"Well, I'll be buggered," declared Clem Abernathy.

"And himself under the sod only the better part of a month," said Elbows McFadden. "Praise be to God."

"Praise be to the now-dead Abner Calisher," muttered Three-Card Monte.

"We'd better drink to the occasion," Bill Forefinger said, and reaching for the bottle he added, "This is big news, my friends! Twins, born of a widow."

"A forty-year-old widow," said Cy Pone.

The news spread through Little Missouri with the speed of the proverbial forest fire. Doc Slattery, who had delivered, was assailed with questions, and finally was called upon to address the large group that had been called together by the Reverend Elihu Burlingame. The congregation now stood—for some unknown reason bareheaded—in the center of the street, halfway be-

116

tween the Sure Shot and the Hotel de Paris, as the reverend addressed them on the wonders of birth, marriage,
America, and also God. Then he led them in prayer.

Meanwhile, the boys from the Sure Shot's back room
had tumbled out into the street and stood with the gaping throng.

Someone wanted to bring the widow outside, with
men carrying her bed so that she could be cheered by
the sight of her happy neighbors, but the idea was voted
down when Doc Slattery pointed out that though the
widow was doing well, she had to be careful, and
shouldn't be allowed to get overexcited.

The Allen, arriving late on the scene, suggested a
parade and a prizefight with himself and Slocum as the
participants for the championship of America. And
someone suddenly said, "We got to do something!"

"What?" somebody else asked.

Three-Card spoke up then, in his take-charge manner. "We got to let people know what's happened here.
This here is like history. It ain't everyday somebody has
twins."

"Not in Little Misery," someone shouted in a sudsy
voice from the back of the crowd. It turned out to be
Willy Hames, the hostler working for Bill Forefinger.

"We got to let people know," Three-Card said. "Send
a telegram!"

"Send it to who?" someone asked.

"We could send it to the President," Three-Card said.

"Maybe Queen Victoria ain't to be overlooked," said
Packy O'Gatty, who like his companions had also par-
taken liberally of the strong grain while at the gaming
table through the night.

"Hell," said Three-Card. "Let's go right to the top.
We'll tell the Pope."

"I think we oughta tell the President," Cy Pone said.

"You don't like the Pope?" shouted The Allen, starting to get angry.

"I love the Pope," Cy countered swiftly. "Greatest man in the whole wide world, but if we don't tell the President he could get sore at us."

It was decided to send the telegram to the President. No one, however, knew what his address should be. Three-Card said why not just send it to Washington. This was accepted by everyone as a good idea and the telegram was sent, announcing Little Muddy's supreme event. After which everyone went back to celebrating.

The Allen was still trying to talk up a prizefight with John Slocum, but the man was nowhere to be found.

"I tolt ya, he's ascairt of me!" The announced to the population of Little Misery.

An hour after the telegram had been sent to Washington, and just as John Slocum rode his Appaloosa back into town and dismounted outside the Hotel de Paris, a telegram was handed to Clem Abernathy, who, in the absence of a mayor, usually took that role when needed.

He read it and handed it to Three-Card Monte Kitchen, who read it and handed it to Elbows McFadden.

"Read it aloud!" somebody shouted.

Elbows, with watering eyes and a quivering mouth read the message aloud: "I am most pleased to learn that at long last a forty-year-old widow in Little Muddy has given birth to twins. But where the hell is Little Muddy? Signed: The President."

"Praise the Lord," sighed Elihu Burlingame, gazing fondly at his "wife's" rump as she climbed up into the Conestoga in search of a bonnet she had brought with her from St. Louis.

Elihu was all for climbing right in after her and getting it—by God—if necessary by force, but he saw John Slocum, still laughing over the telegram, bearing down on him.

Lord, he murmured within, you have deserted me in my hour of need, damn it, God! And he turned a ghastly smile of welcome onto Slocum.

Slocum had also seen those friendly buttocks disappearing into the Conestoga, and could appreciate what was going through Burlingame's mind.

"I wanted to have a word, Elihu."

"Why sure, sure, Slocum. Where'll we go? Afraid Charlie's got the wagon. We could set over yonder if you like." And he nodded to a slight rise of ground about a hundred yards away.

When they had walked far enough away from the wagon and squatted down, Slocum said, "Wanted to ask you about Horatio Kyle. Is he fixing to come out to Little Muddy?"

It had been a wild shot, and he saw it hit Burlingame. But Elihu wasn't a fake reverend for nothing. He didn't react. It was more in the atmosphere that Slocum felt his challenge hit.

Elihu was all sanctity as he said, "Horatio Kyle?" He said the words slowly, carefully, as though tasting them. "I don't believe I know the name. Wait a minute . . ." He held up a hand, as though searching memory, then lowered it, sighing lightly. "No. Thought for a minute he was one of my flock back in St. Louis. But no. I am afraid you have the advantage, sir. I know no one by that name."

Slocum canted his head, squinting an eye at his companion from under the wide brim of his Stetson hat. "Could have sworn you'd know Kyle. One of them skinners, the bigger one—forget his name; the ones we took along on the buffalo hunt—he mentioned the name. It sounded like someone who was coming out here, and I thought from St. Louis. Course, I could have made a mistake. Reckon I did." But he didn't stand up and let it go. He remained, hunkered right alongside the man he had pinned with his question.

A long shot, but he wanted to see if he could shake Burlingame. The man was into something, that was very evident. His story of westering in search of a community where he could start a church and his wife could teach school just didn't ring true anymore.

Slocum felt at an impasse. A lost mine? The Edgertons looking for Uncle Harry's former grave? The skinners and Dutch obviously up to something while under orders of somebody else? Three-Card and his friends taking Lord Frederick and his bankroll for a hayride? Burlingame and Charlie and their strange wagon train, who were obviously not going anywhere, who had obviously arrived at their destination. Little Muddy? And a name: Kyle. Who was he? Nellie had told him that she had quite by chance overheard The Allen mentioning the name to Elihu Burlingame one night in the Stud. She remembered it clearly, for it happened to be a night when The had again tried to get her into bed, and later the same night Elihu had taken the same notion.

"I wouldn't let either one of those scum touch me with a borrowed pecker," she'd said calmly, as though announcing that there was coffee on the stove.

"And you never heard the name again?" he had asked.

"Never. Thing is, I lied to you before on account of I was afraid. I think it was the way they were talking, all hushed up like they didn't want anyone to hear. But I'd come in on them unexpectedly, on account of the door was partly open, and I had to give the evening before's money to The. They looked so damn funny I noticed the name. But when you said it, I didn't catch it at first."

"I got it," Slocum had said. "But how did they actually say it, and what?"

She had studied it a moment. "Like he—that's Kyle —would be here soon. Yes . . ." Her face cleared now, for she'd tensed somewhat trying to recollect the scene. "Yeah. The was saying when will Kyle be here? And the other one, the preacher, he said soon. And then he said, 'Remember that, The. Kyle is coming here to Little Muddy soon. So you be on your good behavior. Don't fuck up.'" She had nodded to herself as she remembered the scene. "That was it. Like that."

And so he had tried it on Elihu, The having left the scene after the reading of the telegram from the President. But while the reverend was admitting nothing, Slocum could see that his question had hit. It was all right. It would stir some action; and it was this that was needed. The strange impasse had been going on too long.

He thought then of the telegram and smiled.

"Did I say something funny?" Elihu asked. "I see you're smiling."

"I was thinking of the telegram," Slocum said. "And how this town, by golly, has got something good."

"Something good?"

"The town knows how to laugh."

He had been watching Charlie as she walked toward them. She was close enough to have heard his last words.

"Who do you think sent the telegram back?" she

asked as she sat down on the grass between the two men.

"Why, the President of the United States," Burlingame said.

"I mean really." She was looking at Slocum. "Did you send it?"

"I wasn't here. I only got into town just as the answer came back."

"But who, then?"

"The town sent it to itself," Slocum said. "How's that?"

"That's too strange for my head," Elihu said, standing up.

All three were up now and had started to walk back toward the wagon and the town.

Suddenly Slocum stopped and turned to face Elihu. "It was someone with a great sense of humor," he said. "It's one of the things that's so good about this here country—people know how to laugh. Take a man like Kyle, he'd get a great kick out of this."

"He'd have laughed his—" Charlie started to say, but her husband cut in, smooth as silk. "Stile, Bert Stile would indeed have laughed his head off, my dear!"

He turned to Slocum, the corners of his eyes and mouth holding tightly to his smile. "A family friend," he said. "An old family friend. Bert Stile."

There were some things that Horatio Kyle appreciated above all else, and one of these was the fabled Cheyenne Club. The fame of this posh watering and dining oasis in the far reaches of Wyoming easily rivaled other such establishments in San Francisco, Kansas City, Denver, and even Chicago. None surpassed the Cheyenne retreat where the great minds and muscle of the frontier expansion came together to relax, to plan, even to share, and, not least, to plot.

The Cheyenne Club boasted the best steward, the best chef, and the best wine cellar of any club in the whole of the United States of America. Far from the hot prairie, the icy reach of mountain winter, the saddle sores and necktie parties and the cowboy grub line, it was just here in these leather armchairs that great oaks from little acorns grew. Here, history—as the saying went—was often made.

Horatio Kyle appreciated more than anything else the fact that he had finally—and after unremitting struggle —made it to the Cheyenne Club. It was surely the fitting symbol of his success, a reminder of how he had built, carved, and, yes—shotgunned—his career into the top brackets. In this he had even surpassed his great teacher, Holy John Swayles.

Holy John, after all, had worked in an earlier time, a less populated place. He had worked the riverboats for years and had then developed his own form of scam, which his ward and pupil had taken as his own, and upon which he had embellished fruitfully. But whereas Holy John never resorted to weaponry, unless under extreme danger, his disciple, while following the older man's example for some years, had finally found it necessary to come to terms with a tougher, less scrupulous society. And this was especially so as he got closer to the top. Here at the top the competition was murderous. However, the rewards were at the very least tremendous.

In the great Chicago cattle scam, for instance, Horatio had to resort to "regulators," just like the big stockmen of the association. Similarly in the Great Diamond Hoax, he'd not only used bribery—usually par for that sort of game—but had improved his position through blackmail, slander, and the ultimate—guns. Not himself, to be sure—he never carried a gun—but through "regulators," as they were politely called. Violence, in short, had become more and more an adjunct to the success of his operations.

When Amelia, the present lady of his need and choice, raised the subject with him he was able to find in himself the adroit answer. He had replied that he only used harsh means when it became necessary to assure that the other party involved saw the situation clearly enough to "do the right thing." Unassailable logic, as Kyle saw it.

There was no question in Kyle's mind as he sat in one of the leather armchairs in the Cheyenne Club that he was doing the right thing in hiring Olive. The man had worked as a cattle detective and regulator, and had performed yeoman's service for the association during the cattle war in northern Wyoming. In fact, Kyle had learned that the man was so proficient at his job that nobody who hired him ever wished to be seen in his presence. Such was Olive's reputation that he was accorded the ultimate accolade: avoidance, the fear of being linked in any way at all with him. Kyle reasoned that Olive had to be a very lonely man, a fact that he marked in his mental file as a possible means of manipulating him.

Originally, during the first drawing of personnel for the plan, he had wanted Stonebraker. It was always good to have a lawman "working with you," and to be seen in his presence, and having handy anecdotes and remarks that could be dropped at strategic points: "As I was saying to Marshal So-and-so," or "As I learn from Sheriff Whatever..." And, too, personal vignettes were always handy for dropping into a conversation: "Yes, for sure that is so. Why, I recollect how Judge Jones had a terrible trouble with his new teeth. . . ."

But he had shortly found out that everything he'd ever heard about Stonebraker was true. The man was not for sale, nor even for hire. Kyle, though, had been smart enough to use an intermediary in the offer so that Stonebreaker had no idea who it was wanted him "for a special job."

So he had turned to Olive; the man was quite a different kettle of fish than Stonebraker, although there were certain gray areas where something of each met the other. After all, he had it on good authority that Stonebraker occasionally had used Olive for certain investigations.

Olive—and nobody knew whether it was his first name or his last—was already a legend. One of the great ones. He had ridden with the Army against Geronimo. He was said to have been a close friend of Blackjack Ketcham. He was a trick rider and roper who had won prizes for his feats—bronc riding, bulldogging, and of course marksmanship. In range warfare he had gained a reputation as a cold-blooded killer, especially after he was charged with murdering a ten-year-old boy, the son of a homesteader, though nothing could be proved.

The man inevitably fought on the side of the cattle barons. A hired gun, as some newspaper writer had succinctly put it. Olive openly boasted how he hated nesters, homesteaders, rustlers, and sheepherders— anyone, that is, who fenced the open range and interfered with the voracious appetites of the cattlemen.

It was obvious to Kyle that Olive was what was needed to ride herd on his crew of gamesmen and women, his gunmen, and all those who would be needed at the moment trouble might arise. Especially if the Indians got into it. Kyle was in for the big money, and he didn't care to risk even the smallest chance of something going wrong.

But—and he felt this was brilliant—he planned not to use Olive overtly. That is, not out in the open. He had heard how Stonebraker had worked with the man, using him on the side of the law. Though it was actually on account of that, according to the report, that the deal broke up. Olive apparently had objected to working too far on the side of the law, as per Stonebraker's requirements.

But Kyle would take a leaf from Stonebraker and use Olive more as a "threat," a means of applying pressure when pressure was needed. And it almost always was.

Subtle, would be the word. Smooth as silk. Surround your opponent, apply the pressure here, there, and then, *snap*! And the trap was shut. For instance: "I'll let Olive handle that one," or "We'll have to see what Olive thinks of it," and "I wonder how Olive will see your point."

Such remarks, well placed, could be most helpful, and avoided the harshness—and worse, the commitment—of the open threat, which of course had to be increased the next time round, and so soon lost power and validity.

Kyle settled back into the big leather armchair, drawing on his cigar. He loved a good cigar. Indeed, he loved good wine, good spirits, and, well, not exactly "good" women, but surely women with all the things he dreamed about when those divine moments appeared in his head—the scenes of lurid action which would either be replays of actual sexual activity or anticipation of pleasures to come. Not as good as the actuality, surely, yet sometimes . . . well, he had a lively imagination.

These fantasies were equaled in his pantheon of day-dreams only by the pictures of himself and the wonders he had wrought from the world of the Wild West. And it was at this precise moment that he recalled yet again the tremendous idea that had occurred to him recently at the Inter-Ocean Hotel when Amelia had come in and inter-rupted him. It was here again, right now at the Cheyenne Club. The new great idea.

The plan unquestionably had a million-dollar ring to it. And the gathering of solid—not to forget affluent—citizens listened carefully as Horatio Kyle brought his points to bear.

"Gentlemen, as you know, we are all flushed with the excitement of the transcontinental railroad finally being completed." And he turned toward one of the five men seated at the round table. "I believe Mr. William Sloane will agree?"

Sloane, a gray-haired man with a trim mustache, a man of perhaps sixty-some years, nodded vigorously, while his companions watched his reaction. These were Haynes Rawling, a private investor; Fletcher Fahnstock, of the Anglo-American Prairie Corporation; Clyde Fitz-simmons, of Montana Mining; and Patrick Dunlittle, of the Bank of California, a retired Army general.

Horatio Kyle looked around the table, smiling quietly. It was the moment he had built to. He leaned forward, his elbows on the table, and the tips of his fingers together, making an arch in front of him.

"But," Kyle resumed, "the excitement has simmered down, and now we face the likelihood of a spur moving south. A long spur. It just so happens that the proposed spur will run through the area of the Little Missouri River. In other words, civilization will come to the north country, and this will open further the Great West . . . with trade, immigrants, cattle, commerce, and"—he held up a forefinger—"gold!"

He had their complete attention. He could feel it, the way a major actor can capture and hold an audience in thrall.

It was William Sloane who was the first to clear his throat. "And I, for one, have heard that you are planning to reopen a mine north of Mandan in the Black Hills."

"I think we've all heard that," Fletcher Fahnstock put in. "Fact is, that's why I'm here, Mr. Kyle." And a rich chuckle fell from his paunchy cheeks. Fahnstock was almost bald, and under the sunlight coming through the window of their private room at the Cheyenne Club, his head shone.

"Quite," replied Kyle. And to himself he thought how well it was working—getting them to talk, to bring up the subject themselves.

"My understanding is that you have an old mine, or an abandoned mine, somewhere near Mandan, Kyle. Is that correct?" It was Haynes Rawling speaking.

"Actually, the Mud River Mine is west of Mandan, near a town—a hamlet, really—named Little Missouri."

"But I understand the Mud River Mine flooded. Up till then, I've been told—and I wouldn't be surprised if all of you gentlemen know it—the profits had run into very big figures." It was Clyde Fitzsimmons speaking, from Montana Mining. "But you've said, Mr. Kyle, that you have a system of pumping out the water. I have heard of it. I just don't know whether it would work in this particular instance. But"—and he sat back, looking around the table—"I'm open to be convinced." And a big grin spread across his face.

Kyle sat comfortably in his chair, relaxed, yet at the same time wholly alert as he unfolded his plan for pumping the water out of the Mud River Mine and resuming operations. Thus the talk continued while they had a superb luncheon, with wine, cigars, and brandy. His guests were comfortable, and he could tell they were listening carefully to his proposition.

"It's of course backing I need, gentlemen. There's a gold mine there. Look at its past record. As I've told you, I have had mining men look everything over with an eagle eye. And I have the new equipment available, just waiting to be shipped when I give them the go-ahead."

He paused while the waiter entered and refilled the wine glasses.

"It's an excellent wine, Kyle," said Patrick Dunlittle of the Bank of California. "It's a pleasure to do business with a man not only steeped in financial acumen, if I may say so, but in cosmopolitan tastes." And he raised his glass to toast their host.

Kyle beamed with the proper amount of modesty, and also the acceptance of what was only his due. After all, Dunlittle was only speaking the truth.

"You each have a copy of the prospectus in front of you, and I hope you will read it carefully. What I propose is that we form a finance group—providing you will want to go ahead with me, and I am sure you will —and get going before the snow starts to fly. I have a whole cadre of mineralogists, geologists, and any other kind of ologist we might need," he ended up laughing. The others swiftly joined him.

The waiter poured brandy. The company was in a more expansive mood now that the cards were on the table. It had taken a lot of convincing to get the men here. But it was now that the most difficult moment would come. The question tugging at Kyle's thoughts was whether someone would now snap at the bait.

"By the way, General," Kyle said, turning toward Patrick Dunlittle. "I've run into some friends of yours, last time I was in New York—Lord Frederick Edgerton and his wife."

"Indeed! How are Freddie and Mil? I haven't seen them in a while."

"I'd read something about them in the *Territorial Enterprise*," Haynes Rawling put in. "Off on a buffalo hunt, I believe."

"Oh, I suspect they're really looking for gold," Fahnstock brought out with a little laugh. "Like everybody else."

"Well," said Kyle, raising his glass. "Whatever they're after, let's drink to their finding it. Be it happiness, health, or one of those mysterious lost gold mines."

"Like the Lost Dutchman," laughed Sloan.

"Or the Lost Ophir."

"What about Massacre Mine?"

The laughter went around the table as they finished their brandy, recounting the usual well-known tales of lost mines.

When the luncheon broke up, it was late afternoon. Kyle said goodbye to them at the door of the smoking room, to which they had moved for a final glass of brandy.

When he got back to his hotel, Amelia was waiting for him. It was already starting to be evening.

"Well, how did it go, darling?" she asked. "You look as though you'd enjoyed yourself."

"Ah, I did. I really did."

"Was the meeting a success? Did they go along with your proposal?"

"Oh, they don't make decisions that quickly. They'll be thinking it over. They have all the information they need. And I should be hearing from them."

"But what do you think?"

They were in the bedroom, and she came now and sat on the arm of his chair with her arm around his neck.

Leaning forward a little, he ran his lips over the back of her hand. "What do I think?"

"Yes. Tell me what you feel about it. You can tell sometimes, can't you? I know I can sometimes tell how the wind is blowing. I mean, someone might have said something that would give an indication, I mean when you give it thought later, afterwards. Do you know what I mean?"

"Oh yes, I do. Indeed I do." A smile was playing at the corners of his mouth. "Only it wasn't anything that anyone said, my dear. But I do think they have, shall I say, caught at the bait."

"How so?" She leaned forward and turned her face so she could look right at him. "Darling, you do look like the cat who swallowed the canary."

His grin took over his whole face now. "Well, it wasn't what anyone said, but what not a single one of them did say that is so interesting. And I must say I broke my back working up the opportunity for it to be said."

"But say what? What was it nobody said?" She was

staring at him, catching his excitement. Yet while she was showing it in her movements and in the sudden coloring in her face, he was quiet; his excitement was much more within.

"Say what?" she repeated, like a little child.

"Only one word."

"One word? Will you please tell me before I go out of my mind with curiosity! You are maddening, Horatio!" And she broke into a laugh, touching the side of his face with her fingertips. "You know, you're like a little boy with your excitement. You can't hide it from me."

"I guess not," he replied, half sheepishly.

"Then tell me what word they never mentioned."

"Why, the most obvious. Coker."

"Coker?"

His grin was all the way across his face. "They mentioned nearly every lost mine in the West; every one of them had some mine he spoke of. But nobody—nobody mentioned the Lost Coker Gold Mine."

9

The afternoon seemed longer than usual, Slocum thought. Or perhaps it was because he felt that expectancy in him. He knew the feeling, but he didn't know what was causing it. It was hot, with the sun burning white as a button in the pale, cloudless sky. He had cleaned his guns, checked the sights on the Sharps and Winchester, and then he'd walked down to the livery to rub up his saddle rigging. Finally he pulled the shoes on the Appaloosa and started nailing on a new set. It was hot work, even though he was working in the slight shade offered by an open-sided shed, but he was enjoying himself. The Appaloosa was standing well, and hadn't given him any trouble so far. Bill Forefinger, the liveryman, came by to say how-de-do and comment on the weather, and later Willie Hames passed some of the time of day with him. But mostly he worked alone with the tough little gelding, cutting, filing, firing up the new shoes, and nailing them on and clinching, and then buffing each hoof, and finally dabbing on linseed.

The Appaloosa stood well for him. He held the front

legs between his thighs and laid the rear legs in his lap. It was hard work, and he was sweating, and it felt good.

He was trimming the last hoof when he felt the change in the atmosphere behind him. Then he saw the shadow of the big man thrown on the ground in front of him, just inside the shed, which was covered with manure and wood shavings. He put down the clippers and picked up the file, continuing to work as though nobody was there.

"Been a while, Slocum." The voice was soft, almost a whisper, but it had a penetrating quality.

"That it has, Olive. It's been a while."

"You takin' up blacksmithin', huh."

"Save a penny and the dollar'll take care of itself," Slocum said.

"Still wearin' your gun cross-draw, huh."

Slocum had his eyes on the man's shadow, and now saw it move as Olive leaned against the post holding up the corner of the open shed.

"I seen Stonebraker," Olive said.

"Always said you had good eyesight, Olive," Slocum put down the Appaloosa's forefoot and straightened up.

He didn't turn around, he walked farther into the shed with the toolbox Willy the hostler had loaned him.

"Want a job, Slocum?"

"I got one."

"Yeah? What?"

Slocum had placed the toolbox on the bench at the back of the shed and now turned and walked out into the sunlight and faced his visitor.

"Mindin' my own business," he said. "You do the same—hear?"

They stood facing each other now, both roughly the same size, though Olive's shoulders were round, as he hooked his thumbs in his gunbelt. He was packing two .44s, both tied low on his thighs, and there was plenty of extra ammo in his belt.

Slocum watched the flush come into Olive's dark face at his words. One of his hands moved away from his belt, then moved back.

"We'll let 'er go till another time," Olive said. "Just wanted you to know I was about."

"I already knew."

"I always said you was smart, Slocum."

"Not smart. I just got a good nose."

Olive's eyes were very dark, maybe black, but they were small so it was hard to tell. But now they seemed to get darker as the angry flush spread in his swarthy face. "Just stay out of my way, Slocum."

"I'll do what I feel like doing, mister. Now bugger off."

Olive's thick lip curled. "I'll be seeing you."

But now Slocum had had enough. He stepped forward, with his hands at his sides, ready for anything. "I don't want to see you, Olive. Except in my gunsight. Now get out of here. You're stinkin' up the fresh air!"

"Our time will come, Slocum."

"Now? You want to try now? You got the guts to try right now?"

The tableau suddenly froze as both came to the lip of settling it. Across the street two small boys were watching from an alley. One was sucking his breath at a great rate, the other's leg was shaking. They stood there rooted to the ground.

Then, without another word, Olive straightened, turned, and walked off down the street.

Slocum led the Appaloosa back into the stable and stalled him. Then he walked on down to his hotel.

When he got there the desk clerk told him he had a visitor in the coffee room.

"I thought you said you didn't want to be seen with me around town," Slocum said as he sat down.

Stonebraker pushed his Stetson hat onto the back of his head. "It don't matter too much by now, I don't reckon. I seen your social chat with Olive there, and figured what it was about."

"It was about him being more worried now than he was beforehand," Slocum said, nodding to the waitress for coffee. "What's on your mind? I don't have too much to tell you. Nothing I could add to what I already told you about my visit to Drover and my talk with that old geezer who used to be the undertaker hereabouts."

"Why do you figger Olive's here?" Stonebraker said, taking a dead cigar butt out of his coat pocket and lighting it.

"Somebody is working something. What it is I don't know, but I think it has to do with the Edgerton's, and it looks like maybe something to do with the uncle's hunting trip out here."

"I was thinking the same."

"Who are you working for Stonebraker? Come on. I've been open with you. Is it the Stockgrowers? If so, I'm backing off. I don't care what trouble you think you can cause me, I don't like those sonsofbitches."

"It ain't the Stockgrowers."

"Who then?"

"Did you know the Northern Pacific is going to activate this track down here?"

"I thought it was already operating."

"That's true, but it ain't making a red cent. See, they laid track, they even got rolling stock operating, but they overlooked one thing: there ain't anything to haul either way. There's no freight. And damn few passengers. Get it?"

"No business, no money. Make business, make money," Slocum said.

"You got the idea."

"How?"

"Simple. You make business so that business can make business. Get it?"

"I get it."

"Then your railroad can haul that business."

"I said I got it."

Stonebraker's stogie had gone out. He cussed under his breath and relighted it. Slocum took another look around the coffee room. It was deserted save for themselves.

"So they need Olive for that, eh?"

"You know I used to use Olive, but on the side of the law."

"You're saying that this time he's working the other side."

"There's only one side to the law, Slocum, and I am him."

"Are you sure you're the only one. The law sometimes works in damn strange ways its wonders to perform." And Slocum looked deadpan at his companion as he took out a quirly and lighted it.

The wolf grin appeared suddenly on Stonebraker's chipped face. "You got an idea what kind of business that railroad is figuring to be hauling?"

Slocum nodded. "I figure it's got to be rated pretty high for them to go to the trouble of laying on a man like Olive."

"It is. It is damn high." Stonebraker's milky eyes looked straight at Slocum now. "You got a notion?"

"I have heard that there are men who will kill for gold."

The wolf grin spread, and the lawman's eyes seemed to Slocum to clear suddenly into a glitter.

"I hope you have also figgered that Mr. Olive ain't visiting here in this godforsaken place just for some pieces of gold. He's got something extra in mind."

"I figgered that about the time I finished shoeing my horse," Slocum said.

"I always figgered you as a man who didn't waste his time dreaming," Stonebraker said as he stood up and adjusted his hat. He stood facing Slocum, who had also risen. "Watch your back, Slocum."

"Olive ain't planning to shoot me in the back."

Stonebraker's wiry eyebrows shot up at that.

"He wants to be top gun," Slocum said. "He has to shoot me in a shoot-out." And then, seeing the doubt in the little lawman's face, he said, "Else the sonofabitch would have done it already."

"I'm telling you, most men are tough a good deal of the time—I mean like them that deals with the law, no matter what side it is. But the rest of the time they're somethin' else. But that Stonebraker, I do believe he's tough all the whole time."

It was Bill Forefinger speaking as the group sat in their favorite back room at the Sure Shot.

"What about Olive?" Elbows McFadden said. "I heard of him. I wouldn't never want to meet up with him."

"Olive is in town," Three-Card said.

"That's what I know." Elbows reached for his glass, and his eyes dropped to his cards.

"Well," Three-Card said, throwing down his cards,

"I can't make it this hand." And he took the cigar out of his mouth. "Let's study it a minute. We got to see where the hell we're at."

Cy Pone pulled in the meager pot, and the boys threw their cards into the pile and sat back.

"It's that Lord and his missus," Three-Card said. "I have the strong notion that they—or anyways *he*— hasn't come all the way out here to hunt flea-bitten buffalo." And he cocked a racy eye at Clem Abernathy, who was seated directly across from him.

Abernathy picked up on it. "You're not suggesting His Lordship and Mrs. Lordship are out here prospectin' for some of that yellow stuff, are you?"

"Well, I'll be buggered!" exclaimed Forefinger. "Who'd of thought it!"

"Looks like about everybody exceptin' you, my lad," Packy O'Gatty said, almost tripping over his brogue with excitement. "I been cogitatin' the very same, Three-Card, wonderin' when you boys would pick up on it."

"But is it true?" Cy Pone put in soberly. "Are we just thinking it, or is it for sure?"

Three-Card Monte Kitchen regarded the proprietor of the Doggone Eatery with an amused look on his face. "We and a whole lot of other people are makin' real horses' asses out of ourselves if it ain't so, by God!"

It was a big moment, Three-Card saw. Elihu had instructed him on how to handle it, and by golly it was working. He told himself now that he had known it would. Elihu didn't know everything, by God. He looked at his companions, their faces loaded with response to the gravity of the situation. He knew that within an hour or two after the meeting broke up the news would have covered the town. Elihu—and himself—knew how to read the cards, by damn!

"But does His Lordship know where the Coker is? I mean, has he got a map or something?" asked Elbows.

"That is not known," Three-Card said. "Cooch, one of the skinners that was with them and Slocum, he seems to think from what he overheard that His Lordship has it in his head maybe."

"In his head!" Cy Pone's voice almost cracked in surprise. "You mean he's got nothing on paper? What I'm asking is does he *know*?"

"Or is he trying to remember somethin' somebody told him?" put in Clem Abernathy.

"I don't know whether he knows or not," Three-Card said, his tone suave in the face of the flurry. "He is looking for his uncle's grave."

"So he says!"

"Hell, the old buzzard wasn't in that grave long enough to warm it, I been told."

"And anyways, the grave ain't the Lost Coker. Do you really think the old man found something, I mean like gold?" Elbows McFadden's voice ended on a solemn note of awe.

"There was gold dust in his fingernails, I have been told." And this firm statement, uttered by Three-Card, quelled any possible objection.

"Jesus." The single word, spoken with reverence in the face of the miraculous, brought the room to a new solemnity. And those present drank.

Shortly, Packy O'Gatty spoke. "So what is our move, boys? Do we try to find out where this bonanza is—I mean start looking for it ourselves?"

"Hell no!" Three-Card's voice came in, harsh with needed reality in the face of the tremendous pipe dreams that were filling the room. "Do you want all the whole of the country out here spoiling it for the rest of us? No sir!"

"But what are we going to do then?"

"We can't just sit on our asses while somebody else finds the Coker!"

"Right. But we don't know where to look!"

"But maybe His Lordship knows," Three-Card pointed out, his words suave with the voice of reason.

"You mean, let him find it and—"

"And then we come in to help him like," said Cy Pone.

"Or maybe we could even get in there ahead..." And Three-Card cocked an engaging eye as he lifted one eyebrow very high on his forehead. "If you can figure what I mean," he concluded.

All drank vigorously now to the future enterprise, whatever that might be, while Three-Card Monte Kitchen relaxed into his hardback armchair, slowly drumming his fingers on the tabletop before him, and reviewed the possibilities that now flowed from the rumor he had instigated.

"We'll get those skinners to keep a tight eye on His Lordship," Three-Card said. "The first sign of anything suspicious, they'll tell us."

"What about Slocum?" O'Gatty asked. "He looks to be closer to that there Lord and Lady than a thread to a needle, as me dad used to say it."

"Slocum too, to be sure," said Three-Card. "And anybody else who might need watching."

"Meanwhile...we wait?" It was Elbows asking the question.

"Meanwhile, not a word to anybody," said Three-Card. "Nothing."

"Don't say nothing to nobody," agreed O'Gatty. "But we'll keep our eyes open."

"And our mouth shut!" added Mr. Kitchen, firmly reaching for his drink. And he smiled to himself, knowing he had guaranteed the exact opposite.

"I was wondering if you would help us," Lady Millecent was saying as Slocum joined her in the parlor car which she and Lord Frederick were still using as their home. The château that the couple hoped to build was still in the planning stage.

"I'll help you with anything I can," Slocum said. "I mean within reason," he added with a smile.

"But of course, Mr. Slocum." And Lady Millecent looked at him thoughtfully as she said those words, as though measuring what else she might say.

Slocum found her absolutely enjoyable, but this did not lower his guard as his ears opened to take in whatever else she would now say to him.

"What is it you want? And, uh, will Frederick be here?"

"I am here," Frederick's smooth English voice preceded him into the parlor car; and he followed with all the freshness of a college sophomore, Slocum thought. He had once guided some young collegiates on a pack trip in the Yellowstone country. They were tenderfeet and a yard wide, as he had told it later, but they were also refreshing, and he had enjoyed their company. As he enjoyed Frederick's. But Millecent's company, on the other hand, was a lot more than simply enjoyable. And he could feel the warmth coming from her even while her husband was there with them. Well, maybe they had an understanding. But that was their business.

"Freddie and I had thought that since you are here—

and if you are available—that we would like to seri-
ously look for where Uncle Harry was buried. I mean,
get up a real expedition."

"We were wondering," Freddie said then, "whether
there would be any value in asking some of the Indians
if they could show us where the fighting took place
where Harry was killed."

"And I've been wanting to ask you something," Slocum said. "Can you tell me—do you know just how, in
what way your uncle was killed?"

"He was killed with arrows, my father told me. It
was he who brought the body back home."

"Did he have any lead in him?"

"Lead?" Millecent asked.

"Bullets."

"I never heard that," Freddie said. "I always heard
that he had a whole lot of arrows in him."

"But you know, when you're young, as you were,
and you hear of Indians, you naturally think of bows
and arrows. Right?"

"But of course," Millecent said. "That's natural."

"He might have been killed by being shot."

"What exactly are you saying?" She was leaning forward now, almost on the edge of her chair, her eyes
intent on Slocum.

"Maybe he wasn't killed by Indians at all," Slocum
said. "Maybe he was shot by white men."

"But my God!" exclaimed Lord Frederick. "How?
Why? Whatever for?"

"Maybe the gold mine you say he mentioned in his
letter."

"But, but I thought we'd all thought that was a figure
of speech, not an actual gold mine!"

"I am saying maybe it was an actual gold mine. But I repeat—maybe."

"Well, I'll be blowed!" Lord Frederick was at once returned to being a puzzled schoolboy.

"That *is* a rum go," Lady Millecent said, with a shocked smile as she looked at Slocum. "Do you really think that might have happened?"

"My God," murmured her husband.

"I don't know. I'm only mentioning it as something to take into account."

"Will you help us?"

"Lady, I thought that's what I'd been doing for the past half hour. And even, for that matter, the past several days."

Frederick broke into a shout of laughter at that. "Have you got that, lady!" he roared. "Slocum, you're a dose of salts for us."

Millecent was smiling happily through her flushed embarrassment, and he thought she looked adorable.

"But my heavens, Mil," exclaimed Frederick. "What ever would we do with a gold mine!"

"Darling," and she smiled beautifully, Slocum thought. "We'll spend it."

She had a long nose, long legs, and low-slung breasts which he adored. Whenever Kyle saw her he was overcome with desire. And yet whenever he looked at Amelia in a certain way—as when he would look at each part separately—he saw that by the usual standards she was quite ordinary. What was it, then? The whole greater than its parts? That wasn't enough to explain his passion, and not only that, his . . . yes, his fondness. Did he love her? Was he in love with her? It never occurred to him to ask himself. Perhaps then it was her air, her atmosphere, simply the way she moved, smiled, looked at him. Not overlooking—oh, no—the fantastic way she made love. Horatio Kyle even wondered at such moments as the present, with these thoughts running through him, whether he trusted her.

"You see, my dear, there are two ways of approaching everything, two large, main ways, and of course several small avenues within those major ways."

"Darling, it all seems so terribly involved and complicated. I'm sorry, but I'm not a—let's say—a sort of general of an army as you are."

They were lying naked on the wide double bed, looking up at the ceiling, following their lovemaking. Kyle had been showing her one of his trophies—the Grandine catalogue, the gambler's bible, with its array of unique advantage tools: the holdouts, shiners, trimmers, marked cards, the cut dice all offered to the professional by the great supplier. And, one must add, the most reliable and well known. The volume at hand had been Holy John's, and Kyle had taken it as his inheritance, a "family Bible."

Amelia was happy. She felt him at this moment as a small boy showing off his treasures. And she snuggled even closer to him. "I'm sorry, darling, if I seem stupid, but I really am interested in what you tell me. It's just that I don't see why you don't make things simpler. Am I being dumb?" And she raised up on an elbow and looked down at him out of her large eyes, while her great nipple on her right breast tickled along his chest.

"I can explain it," Kyle said, his organ beginning to stir again. "But I don't want to bore you."

"Tell me," she said, lying back. "And then you can bore me with your lovely penis."

"I could do that now."

"We have all night, you said."

"That's right, I did say, so we won't rush it."

"You told me you were going to make lots and lots of money and then we'd go to Europe and travel and live happily ever after."

"I've always wanted to go to Monte Carlo," he said. "Where would you really want to go?"

"Wherever you are."

"You see, like I was trying to tell you before I got distracted . . ."

"I'm sorry . . ."

"There are two ways of dealing with a problem, or planning something. One is to play out all the detail in advance, figuring each detail, rather like a mathematics situation."

"That sounds most sensible to me."

"The only trouble is that that situation, that method rather, doesn't take into account enough of the human factor. People. And the fact that once the action starts it then influences your developing plan. The plan then has to be changed or modified, as you get back material on how events are going."

"Of course."

"Now, some people lean more on one method, and some on the other. Most people prefer the heavily planned, or even over-planned method."

"Why?"

"Because they feel more safe with a plan, with something really definite."

"But of course. I certainly would."

"But the other method . . ."

"Your way."

"Not wholly," he argued. "But, well I do emphasize it, because when one accepts that method one is more open to change, to surprise, to the unexpected. One can improvise. Like an artist. Like a great artist," he concluded, remembering how Holy John used to put it.

"I see. Well, anyway, the best one is the one that works, after all, isn't it?"

He grinned at the ceiling. "It is, my dear."

She was silent, but he knew she hadn't fallen asleep.

"You see," he went on. "It really is extremely simple."

"I wish you would explain it, sir," she said with a laugh. "I am all ears."

"It's the old dipper's trick. You distract everybody's attention in one direction, and while they're taken, you slicker them from their blind side. Just like a dip does."

"What the hell is a dip?"

"A pickpocket. It's a city expression. I picked it up in Chicago."

"Is that what you're doing?"

"There are only two people who know what I'm doing, my dear. One of them is me."

"And the other?"

He pointed to the ceiling.

She looked at his pointing finger as her hand reached down to his legs. "You've got something else pointing up, I see," she whispered into his ear as she rolled over on top of him, letting his bone-hard shaft sink into her soaking bush.

William Sloane of the Northern Pacific was of course all for the plan. And he told Kyle that, with the opening of the Mud River Mine, business would come swiftly to life as far as his railroad was concerned. But how much Sloane could influence the others was not yet evident.

Horatio Kyle was waiting in the Cheyenne Club on

the clear, sparkling bright morning in June when Fletcher Fahnstock of the Anglo-American Prairie Corporation and Haynes Rawling, the investor, came to call.

"We had a question, Rawling and I," Fahnstock said, after they were seated in one of the smoking rooms. "But first, are we really private here, Kyle?"

"Absolutely. I guarantee it."

Fahnstock, a portly man with a toothbrush mustache, tapped the side of his stubby nose with his forefinger. "It is clear to us that your proposition will help Sloane's Northern Pacific, aside from any gold that is mined at Mud River, all kinds of business will come to Little Missouri, and certainly other towns can spring up along the way. The Northern Pacific can't help benefiting. But much, if not everything, depends on the mine. Right?"

"Right." Kyle smiled at his two visitors and offered cigars.

As the room began to fill with smoke, Haynes Rawling took up the conversation. "Let me put it this way, Kyle. And I believe I'm also speaking for Fletcher here. Actually, we've been hearing a lot about the lost mine, the one that some old prospector or hunter or someone discovered a good many years back. And since he was killed, apparently by the Sioux, no one followed through. No one could find the mine, though I understand many people tried." He paused, his eyes querying his host.

"You are suggesting I might know something about this lost mine? Are you referring to the Coker—" Kyle stopped abruptly as he said the name, flushing a little as though the word had escaped him without his wishing.

"I see you do know it," Fahnstock said, leaning forward.

"I must admit, well, no, not *admit* . . . I mean to say, everybody's heard of the Lost Coker Mine. But, well, it's lost."

"But there are people actively looking for it again. We—Rawling and I—have been talking this whole situation over, and we do feel that you might know something about the Coker."

Kyle could hardly control the bounce that came into his heart as the two men began nibbling at the bait. He put on his most innocent face as he said, "I am not a mining expert, gentlemen. But I must admit, for I am sure you will have heard, since you have gone this far, that, yes, I have had some engineers and government geologist and surveyor investigating. Both men worked for me on the Mud River project when I first considered pumping out the water and reopening the main shaft."

"What did they find?"

"Nothing. As far as I am concerned, gentlemen, the Lost Coker Mine is lost."

A silence fell.

Presently, Kyle spoke. "But this can't possibly affect your feeling about the Mud River Mine."

"Of course not," Fahnstock answered quickly, as though expecting the question.

"No, of course not," added Haynes Rawling.

And Horatio Kyle beamed all through his tight body, knowing that he had them.

"Will you be pursuing any investigation of the Lost Coker?" Fahnstock asked after a long moment had passed.

"I don't see any reason to."

Haynes Rawling took a pull at his glass then. He settled back in his chair and drew on his cigar. He was definitely much firmer now than he had been. He leaned forward with his elbows on his knees. "You understand, I am sure, Kyle, that with so much money involved we—and we have also spoken to Dunlittle and Fitzsimmons, and they are in agreement—with so much involved we've investigated the whole situation pretty deeply in the past two weeks since we met for luncheon."

"I fully expected you to do just that, gentlemen."

Fletcher Fahnstock's smile couldn't hide the fox as he now said, "In the course of our investigations we happened, quite by chance, to discover that you had purchased certain lands, uh, through a Reverend Burlingame."

"Oh yes. For his church, and for his wife's school," Kyle said easily.

"It happens to be a section of land pretty far from town," Rawling said, with a smile in one corner of his mouth.

"The town is expected to grow." Kyle opened his arms, beaming at his visitors. "Gentlemen, what are you driving at? Please come to the point. We're friends here, after all."

"Of course. Of course." Fahnstock held up his hand. He threw a glance at Rawling and then resumed. "You understand, if we—not only Rawling and myself, but the others too; and I said that we had talked it over together, the five of us, including Sloane—if we put money into this venture, well, it will not be a small investment."

"Think of the return, gentlemen. Pennies transformed into dollars. The miracle of finance."

Haynes Rawling's tone was soft, but no less penetrating as he said, "The land we are speaking of, on which we understand you have made an offer, with an agreement on first refusal, happens to be in the same area where the Lord Frederick Edgerton and his wife, along with a man named Slocum, are presently interested; their interest being to find where and how Edgerton's uncle was killed by Indians some years ago."

Kyle said nothing. He was leaning back in his big armchair with his fingertips arched and touching his lips, while watching intently the progress of the conversation.

"Oh, I've heard that story," Kyle said, wearily spreading his hands out in front of him. "About the uncle, I mean. I don't know anything about Lord Frederick and whoever this man is that you mention."

"But you know Lord Frederick," Fahnstock said. "Don't you?"

"Casually. What I am saying is I don't know his business."

His two visitors exchanged looks then, and Fahnstock's head gave a slight nod to his companion.

"We would like to make a proposal to you, then," Haynes Rawling said. "Are you absolutely sure that nobody can overhear us in this room?"

Horatio knew that never in his life had he felt this calm, cool, and collected as he sat before the two men and waited for the proposition he knew was coming.

"The art of the game," Holy John had told him over and over again, "is that not for a single instant must you think of victory, for this brings exultation, and its consequent disasters, for the fine attention to detail has been lost, and the coolness of distance, which you must maintain at all costs, has dissolved; and you are trapped in your own exultation of success. You must remember one thing: it is a *game*!"

Horatio remembered. And after he had listened carefully to the proposal he said only that he would like time to think it over.

10

"Christ sakes, you got more people runnin' around lookin' for the Lost Coker than a dog's got fleas, fer Christ sakes!" Harelip Schneider stared into the corners of the dank, dark, dismal saloon. It was early morning. "They're all out huntin' gold, that's where they be," he snarled at the tall man leaning against the bar.

John Slocum sipped his cup of coffee.

"I hear you got some buffs for His Lordship and his missus," Harelip went on.

"Got a couple," allowed Slocum.

"People figgered you was all lookin' for the mine."

Slocum grinned. "Well, you forget yesterday was the Fourth of July. Everybody's got a head big as a hoss, and I'd say they were sleeping it off."

"Reckon that's why you're drinkin' coffee, eh?" And Harelip grinned, revealing wide areas of gum and few teeth.

"I was lookin for the reverend," Slocum said. "Have you seen him about?"

"He was here a minute ago. Believe he just stepped

out, or"—he threw his eyes toward the upstairs balcony —"maybe up." Harelip sniffed and wiped his nose with the back of his hand. "How's the coffee?"

"Tastes like panther piss."

"Good! I was afraid you wouldn't like it. Say, what you think of all this gold fever? Huh. I don't believe there's a lost mine. I do believe it's all to get up the prices of the land with the Northern Pacific fixin' to come through."

"Where did you get that notion?" Slocum asked, his eyes watching the room in the big mirror in back of the bar.

"Hear people talkin'."

A coughing laugh came from the balcony, and Harelip said, "That's the reverend now, I do believe."

"Leading morning prayers, no doubt," Slocum said as he turned to watch Elihu descending the stairs, a big smile on his face as he saw Slocum.

"How did you know I wanted to see you, Slocum? You must have heard my prayers."

"I heard them bedsprings twanging, Reverend," Slocum said.

"Ah, the music of the spheres! Indeed! I'll take a whiskey, Mr. Schneider." And as they turned toward a table at the far end of the room he said, "Touch of the ague, Slocum."

"Who is Horatio Kyle?" Slocum asked as soon as they were seated.

"Never heard of him."

But the response came too fast. Slocum had seen Elihu's eyes glaze over at the mention of the name.

"That's bullshit, Elihu. Just as much bullshit as you being a preacher. Come on now, cut it out. You know a man named Olive?"

Elihu Burlingame was having trouble. For some reason, Slocum's straightforward approach had shaken him. Until now the big man had treated him as a reverend, with respect. While now it wasn't that he was disrespectful or threatening, but there was definitely a no-nonsense attitude right there.

"I don't know either of those men," Elihu said lamely, and he reached for his whiskey.

"Elihu, I spotted you as a fake a long while ago. Now I want you to come clean with me. Somebody's been spreading rumors about the Lost Coker Mine, that maybe it's been found, or maybe people are looking for it, and that's getting the town and the country hereabouts all spurred up. I want to know who's at the bottom of it."

"Slocum, I swear—I swear on the Good Book! I don't know, and that's the honest-to-God truth. I don't know a thing about what you're talking about."

Slocum studied him a minute, marking the agitation in the man's eyes, his hands, which held his glass of whiskey as if he was afraid of dropping it.

Then he said softly, "Charlie seems to know. In fact, she does know."

"You been talkin' to Charlie?"

"Talking? Uh, yes, in a way of speakin'. Yeah, we've been talking."

He watched the color vanish from Elihu's face as he pushed the knife in slowly and twisted it.

"Why that little bitch!"

"Don't blame Charlie. You're in a jam, mister. And you've got Olive on your hands. I believe he's been after Charlie too."

This bit of news hit him even harder. Slocum was throwing wild guesses, but he had decided it was the time. Somebody had been spreading rumors about the Lost Coker, about the Mud River, about the Northern Pacific, even about the law maybe moving into the area with a bunch of deputy marshals—that last was a wild one he'd heard in The Allen's place. The Allen, meanwhile, had challenged him again to a bareknuckle fight to the finish. But Slocum had told the big bruiser that he was getting tired of beating up on him and that he'd better go out and get a reputation first.

Elihu had been staring down at his hands, which were holding his glass of whiskey. Now he looked up, his long face pale with anger as he fought to control himself. "I don't believe a word of what you say, Slocum. You are the Devil's work, man!" He hissed the last words.

"Ask Charlie. I'll go with what she says."

"What do you mean, you'll go with what she says?"

"If she says I'm telling it straight, then I'll go with it. If she says I'm not, then I'll go with that. She's for you to straighten out, mister." And as he got to his feet, he gave it one more turn. "But watch out for Olive. Olive isn't a nice feller like me."

It was afternoon when Elihu Burlingame finally left the Sure Shot. He had spent much of the day looking for Charlie, who, along with the child, Sarah, had evidently disappeared. Elihu spent his time drinking and going out to look every now and again, and then returning to the saloon. He assumed they had gone for a walk, or possibly Charlie was seeing someone about her proposed school, or maybe she'd even been minding some children. Or—and he burned at the thought—perhaps she was with Slocum. But with Sarah along? No, he didn't think she would do that. Besides, Slocum could have been lying. He was sure Slocum was lying. The man had been trying to stir him up; that was it. So that he'd make a mistake and say something he shouldn't.

Elihu had taken on a good deal of whiskey and now lay down in a field not far from the town, deciding to rest. He was tired, for he had walked a good distance looking for Charlie—down by the creek, over by the low benchland, and around the town, too, at the eatery, the hotel restaurant, and wherever he thought she might have gone. Along the way he stopped in at The Allen's, talked with The, and took on some more whiskey.

He knew he shouldn't. Kyle knew his weakness, and he knew it himself; and both had agreed before he came out on the job that he would have to watch it. Well, he told himself, he was watching it. And he found himself chuckling. He was watching each drink he took. And the notion made him laugh.

How long he slept in the field he didn't know, but the day was still hot when he woke up. He was still tired, but though he wanted another drink he decided not to go into one of the saloons, for he didn't want to talk to anybody. The thought came that maybe Charlie was back at the wagon by now.

She wasn't. And so he pulled out a bottle of whiskey and had a drink—watching it, as he'd promised Kyle, and chuckling at his ruse—and then he lay down again and slept, this time on his bed.

He awakened when he heard her climbing into the wagon. "Where's the kid?" he asked.

"I left her with some people. They had a couple of small ones and an older girl Sarah liked."

He stood in front of her, towering over her, for she was seated on her bed, which was on the floor of the wagon.

"You bitch, I ought to whip your ass!"

"What's the matter with you? You been drinking?"

"You've been with that sonofabitch Slocum."

"No such luck, damn it. Elihu, shut up. You give me a pain, and you know where."

"You been with Slocum!"

"I have not."

"I oughta whip your ass!"

"Don't you touch me! Damn it, Elihu, you remember you're supposed to watch your drinking!"

"I did watch it, my love!" And he roared with laughter. "I watched each and every drink. And you can tell that to Kyle! God damn you and your precious ass! And God damn Kyle! Fuck Kyle! You're supposed to watch your drinking too!"

"Keep your voice down!"

"I will speak as loud as I like, and by God if you don't like it, you can go running to Horatio Kyle and tell him, and you can go screw John Slocum. Or—or you can have me. Here, take a look at this." And he ripped open his fly and pulled out his erection.

She screamed and plunged out of the Conestoga, falling onto the ground as she missed her step in the dark, tripping over a singletree. She was up in a moment and running, while Elihu shrieked curses after her, but he remained in the wagon. She was grateful for the dark. Only, the next thing she knew she had crashed right into someone.

"Slow down, he isn't following you."

Although she couldn't see his face because it was almost pitch dark, she recognized Slocum's voice.

"Let me go," she said.

"I want to talk to you."

"I have nothing to say."

"I think you do. I heard him in there. I heard both of you."

She stared up at him, putting it together. "You set it up! You got him riled up and gave him drinks and worked on him, then you followed and waited."

She relaxed suddenly, and he loosened his hand on her arm.

"Go if you want to," he said. "I'm not the law."

She was holding her head in her hands and shaking it a little from side to side.

At last she said, "I haven't done anything."

"I'm not saying you have. And if you had, it isn't my business. But I do have one question."

"Yes?"

"Do you know Horatio Kyle?"

"Sure I know him. What's that to you?"

"Where does he hang out?"

"In Washington, D.C. What else do you want to know?"

"Tell me about him," Slocum said, knowing what was coming, but playing out the hand.

"He's a man about a hundred years old, with a six-foot-long green beard, three legs, and he eats spiders, little boys, and smart-ass cowboys. Now, excuse me."

"I'd like to see you again."

"I might think about that. But not right now. God-damn it, Slocum, I got to get back in that wagon and put out the fire you started!"

And she turned and ran back to the Conestoga. He could just make out her vague outline as she clambered up into the wagon.

Slocum was saddling the Appaloosa down at the livery when Willie Hames, the hostler working for Bill

Forefinger, called down from the loft where he'd been forking hay.

"Man coming."

Slocum tightened the cinch on the Appaloosa. "He got a name?"

"The law, is his name, and he's packing a hog-leg about as big as himself."

Slocum grinned as the Appaloosa swelled his belly, and he tapped him with the back of his hand until the swelling went down. "Still trying that old trick, eh?" he said softly. "Well, you ain't gonna dump me on my ass on account of a loose cinch, mister."

He was ready, too, when the horse swung his head back and tried to bite his arm as he pulled up on the cinch strap, smacking him in the mouth, but not making the mistake of hitting the animal's teeth as he had done once as a small boy back in Georgia. He had never forgotten that moment, and how his father and brother Robert had laughed at his cut and bruised knuckles.

"You looking for me?" he asked the shadow that fell through the open door.

"I ain't lookin' for that fine-lookin' horse of yours."

Slocum turned to face Stonebraker's lined face, his sprouting eyebrows, mustache, and the wiry hairs flying out of his nose; and mostly his easy-as-pie manner, which fooled everybody except those who knew better.

"I see you got company," the lawman said, nodding toward the loft.

"We'll go out back." Slocum slipped the bridle off the Appaloosa, lifted a halter over his head, and tied him with a loose horse knot to the feed rail. Then he turned and started toward the rear of the barn. Stonebraker followed, spitting at a scampering pack rat but missing.

Behind the barn there was a one-holer outhouse and a round horse corral. There were no horses out, and they walked into the corral and squatted, facing each other, the way they did in that country.

"There's no law up in this country," Stonebraker said, looking down at the lines he was drawing in the dirt with a piece of wood he had picked up.

"By golly, how did you figure that?" Slocum said, staring at him in surprise, with his tongue pushing his cheek out to make a ball.

"I ain't a crack lawman on account of bein' stupid," Stonebraker said, his tone dry as a bleached bone, and he lowered one eyelid at his companion, keeping the other raised.

"What you're saying is that the deal, whatever it is, can be pulled and everyone can be to hell and gone by the time any law gets its ass moving."

"You said it exactly just like the way I would of said it. And that'll be too late. Listen, Slocum. Somebody is pulling one helluva big swindle. Now, tell me something, is there or is there not a Coker Mine?"

"How the hell do I know?"

"You were out with Edgerton and his wife hunting buffalo, but you also been nosying around, and I'm betting my hard-earned money that they've hired you to look for that mine that maybe Edgerton's uncle found— or maybe just knew about."

"That's more or less correct. Fact is, I was about to ride out when you came by."

"Then why in hell didn't you tell me? We're supposed to be working together, remember?"

"I work better alone, Stonebraker."

"I want to know what you're doing."

"I'm squattin' here talking to you."

"Don't be funny!" He spat at a small stone. "Where were you going to look?"

"Up above the Triple K outfit, on the north fork. Edgerton spoke of a pair of towers. Well, first I thought it might be buttes, but I'm thinking now it might be some big rocks his uncle saw, or some kind of high ground. And I heard that the country up yonder looks some like that."

The lawman sniffed, scratched under one arm, and then blew his nose between his fingers, turning his head just slightly away from Slocum.

"Tell me what you've been doing," Slocum said. "I haven't seen you about. You been down to Drover?"

Stonebraker's forehead wrinkled in honest surprise at this. "Glad to see how close you're with it," he said. "Yeah, I went to the land office, the bank, and the telegraph office."

"Did you find out anything on Kyle?"

"Kyle has been meeting with some big men down in Cheyenne, and he's got a passel of people working for him in and around Little Misery. You've likely figured that already."

Slocum nodded.

"The rumor is that someone—most likely Kyle will have a man in front—will be reopening the Mud River Mine, what was flooded some years back and had to close down. The plan is to get special pumps and get the water out. It seems the vein was real good before the flooding stopped the work."

"But he needs capital," Slocum said. "Backing. And not just money."

"Now then . . ." Stonebraker began to draw again with his piece of wood. "The railroad, the Northern Pacific, which has racked up goose eggs in dollars down this way, stands to make big dollars running freight again. Plus, whoever owns property along the line is going to benefit. Businesses can even come there, and this will in turn bring money to the Northern Pacific."

"And you found out at the land office that someone had been buying up land along the railway."

"Guess who?"

"I'd say several names—but one brain behind them. But has he laid out the money, or is it still only on paper?"

"Bull's eye. You know, you'd make one helluva good lawman."

"That is what I know, Mr. Stonebraker," said Slocum with a grin. "And so would you, sir."

Stonebraker broke out laughing at that.

"And the Coker? I'll bet you visited Mr. Arnot Amunsen."

"He's quite a boy. But he couldn't help me much." The lawman took out a quirly and lighted it. Then he resumed. "So I got to admit I'm a bit stuck here. I don't see where the Lost Coker fits in." And he cocked his head at Slocum, who was also lighting a quirly.

"How does this sound?" he said. "It's going to be tough getting anyone to reopen the Mud River, I mean of course the backing, the money. It's a big risk. But the railroad does benefit. That's guaranteed at least for a while. But who knows how long the vein would last?"

"So the Coker is the bait?" said Stonebraker.

"It was the bait maybe in the first place, though that detail doesn't matter—I mean whether he started with the Coker or with the Mud River. In either case, he just about can't lose. His whole play is to not sign anything, not commit himself to anything. See, all this rumor about the Coker: Kyle will have let those mucky-mucks

from the banks and all convince *him* that the Coker is
there."

"That's how the slicker works."

"That's how they all work. But this boy is big, and
he's bolder than new brass, and he's—he's damn good.
He's got everybody all churned up, running around
wondering whether the Mud River will open, wondering
if the Lost Coker can be found. All with their hands out.
Except Mr. Kyle, who lets them convince him that they
should buy into his business, even though they're not
sure what it is."

All the time he was speaking Stonebraker was nodding his head, the wattles at his neck flying about like
loose sails.

"I'd bet my last dollar he's never once said he knew
where the Coker is. But they don't believe him. They're
buying into the Mud River because he's slickered them
into thinking he knows where the Coker is. All he's got
to do is get them to insist on it being in their agreement
that should any of them—including Kyle, of course—
should any one of them hear of anything, or find anything, or learn the whereabouts of the Lost Coker Mine,
then they are all partners."

"You mean he's not even thinking in terms of the
Mud River working out. He'll take the money and vamoose."

"Legally. He'll vamoose legally. The man is an ace,
I'd say."

After a long pause, Stonebraker raised his head to
squint at Slocum from beneath the brim of his Stetson
hat.

"It's the way I've been thinking. Now tell me, where
do the Edgertons fit into the picture?"

"Everyone figures they came out here to look for the

mine—that the uncle had found it, and that's why the Indians killed him. I even heard one story going around that there weren't any Indians, but that the man was shot and arrows were shot into him after he was dead to make it look like Indians did it."

Stonebraker's wolf grin appeared as they both got to their feet.

"Are you saying Edgerton and his missus aren't part of Kyle's game?"

"I don't think they are. But he met them in the East, and apparently urged them to come on out here. So they're a part in that sense, yes."

"Excepting they don't know it, is what you're saying."

Slocum nodded. He took off his hat and replaced it on his head, then squinted at the sun. "They'll be waiting for me," he said.

"The Edgertons."

They walked back into the livery, and the coolness felt good after the hot noonday sun in the bare corral. Stonebraker lighted another quirly while Slocum slipped the bridle onto the Appaloosa and tightened the cinch after adjusting the saddle blanket.

"You're still watching your back trail, Slocum."

Slocum stepped into the stirrup as he grabbed a handful of mane and the reins in his left hand, swung up and over the cantle of the stock saddle. The Appaloosa snorted and twitched one of his ears at a deer fly.

"That's how I saw you coming just now," Slocum said, looking down at the man of the law.

"I'm also talking about Olive."

"That's what I know."

"He's out to build his reputation—at your expense.

It's good for his business, and he's a man likes to spread himself."

"I'm expecting him," Slocum said. "And where will you be?"

"Thought I might take a swing down by Cheyenne."

"Good enough."

"And what'll you be doing out there with Lord Frederick and Lady Millecent?" The wolf grin was stronger than ever as Stonebraker said those words.

Slocum grinned back at him, but his grin was as innocent as a mountain spring. "Why, I'll be looking for the Lost Coker. You don't think I'm bamboozled by all that fancy talk we just went through, do you?"

And their laughter rang into the street of the little town as Slocum kicked the Appaloosa into a brisk canter, heading out to the trail where he was meeting the Edgertons.

It was a fine day, and he watched the sunlight on the far brown hills, wondering suddenly and totally unexpectedly how long those hills had been there, and how long they would remain. Yet the thought was only on the edge of his mind. He was not a man to get caught and lost in thoughts. He was a man who lived by his wits, by the gun, and mostly by paying attention. He knew he could expect Olive anytime now.

"When the game is going against you, the only thing to do is to cut your losses and get out." Kyle often thought of Holy John's injunction. It had always been part of any plan he'd made, any activity he'd engaged in, to have not one but even two or three ways out. You never knew; and this was something Holy John Swayles had drilled into his eager disciple.

At the moment, however, the advice was not pertinent to the situation. At the moment he was riding high, wide, and definitely handsome. And also at the moment, he was standing in front of the big mirror in the smoking room at the Inter-Ocean Hotel in Cheyenne, admiring his fine figure.

Well, he was just back from the Cheyenne Club, having let his five "marks" talk him into including the possibility of the Lost Coker in their deal. He had struggled, had given in reluctantly, urging them to think it over to be sure that that was what they really wanted, because the last thing he wanted to do was even suggest, even hint that such a discovery could be possible. And he told them that he simply could not accept their throwing their money away. But they had insisted to a man. There was no resisting them without coming out and being rude and offending them.

A tremendous moment.

And just for now, just for a few minutes, he indulged himself in another of his favorite pastimes—the telling and retelling to himself the scene of his great play. This particular gambit, however, was his peak achievement. Holy John would have been proud of him. And by the Great Horn Spoon, he had to admit, even though he was a modest man, that he had done it. By George, and by God he had done it!

But then he caught himself, remembering that now, with success in his grasp, was the most dangerous time. It was so easy to let down and thus miss some detail— and a detail that might prove to be vital. No, he must not let down. And anyway, it wasn't all settled. The big shots had been handled—Sloane, Fahnstock, and the others. But there was still Slocum. And Stonebraker sniffing about. Why the hell didn't that crazy old coot go and find some honest way of making a living instead of always pushing the law. No, maybe he'd leave Stonebraker to Burlingame or some other. But Slocum was dangerous. Slocum, he had heard—and he believed it—was the sort of rare type who couldn't be handled. There was only one thing to do with him, and he had done it: Olive was already on his way back to Little Missouri. And Kyle was glad it had been settled. He had enjoyed the meeting with Olive, but it had taken his best effort.

To begin with, the man had barged in as though he thought he owned the place. Well, he had taken care of that right away, had put Olive in his place. It was easy enough. Money. He had offered the man a ridiculously low price, to put him in his place, but then had relented. And he had told him that the job had to be done right away. Kyle didn't care how. Slocum was much too close to the Edgertons, and the whole business could blow up. Of course, he hadn't mentioned anything like that to Olive. All Olive knew was that the price he'd been paid by the Stockgrowers' Association would be handsomely increased, plus there was the possibility of a bonus if it all went smoothly.

"But you must be absolutely careful that no one—I repeat, no one—knows you have any connection with me."

Olive had sat in his chair looking darkly at him.

"Do you understand me?"

Olive had nodded.

"I said, do you understand me?"

"Yeah. Yeah, I unnerstand you."

"I of course have others who could do the job, but I am offering it to you because I understand you have a, uh, personal interest in, shall we say, taking care of this Slocum."

"I'll take care of him. Don't worry. I'll handle him."

"Without anybody knowing your connection with me. I want that to be absolutely clear."

"I'll handle it."

"As soon as possible. You'd better leave for the Little Missouri right away."

"Give me some money. I can't get there for free."

"I'll give you this," Kyle had said, opening a case that was on the table beside him. "For the first payment. The rest you will receive immediately following the successful execution of your task."

"You mean when he is dead."

"Exactly."

The brute had taken forever to count the money, laboring over the crisp bills and licking his fingers and muttering to himself.

"One point, and this is important: afterwards you must get rid of the gun. Throw it in the river, but get rid of it. I'll get you a new one. Here." And he had handed over more money. "We must be very careful that no one suspects you."

Olive had looked at him in surprise, and almost as though he'd been offended.

And then Kyle had said, "I see what's going through your mind. But I don't want any glory gunfight, no shoot-out. I want you to kill him without anyone knowing you did it."

"I can outdraw that sonofabitch."

"I am sure you can, but I want it done this way. The point is that nobody must know who killed him. Look, Olive, you've done work for the association and for other big outfits. I know you have, and you have a clean, honest reputation of turning in a good job. A first-class job. That's all I want. Remember, there's a bonus. If you mess this up you'll be losing a lot of money."

Olive had sat there in the chair, silently turning it over. Kyle could almost read his thoughts. The damn fool wanted to be a top gun, talked about and all that. The idiot!

"Let me tell you something, Olive. The man who is *really* top gun lives a long time, and he doesn't have to be looking behind him all the time. But the man who only has the reputation—he's a target. Look at what happened to Mulligan at Dodge. And I could name others. You pull this job right and I'll have lots of work for you."

Finally the big man seemed to uncoil himself from the chair, and he rose. He was over six feet, but lithe, smooth in his movements. Kyle was impressed, though still not caring at all for his attitude. All brawn and no brain, he'd been thinking. But Olive was what he needed. At the same time it was necessary for him to have an extra ace up his sleeve.

After he had let Olive out of the smoking room and seen him to the front door, he returned, threw open the window, and then lit a fresh cigar.

He stood in the center of the room, looking down at the ash forming on the end of his cigar as he held it in front of him. When the knock came at the door he looked up and said, "Come in."

The man who had entered was dressed in buckskin, and his face was almost entirely covered with hair. He could have been any age between forty and sixty. It was impossible to tell. Yet he moved with a youthful vigor.

Kyle had taken the envelope out of his inner pocket and handed to his visitor. "This is for Burlingame," he said. "And only for him. Not for his wife or anyone else. If anything goes wrong, destroy it. And then return here immediately."

"Gotcha."

"You saw him?"

"Caught him coming in and going out."

"He saw you?"

"No. Neither time."

"How do you know he didn't?"

"He couldn't of. I was hid."

"You're sure."

"I'm sure."

"You have your instructions. Don't let him see you. Or anyone else for that matter. But get that to Burlingame as soon as possible. You've got your money, and there'll be the rest when you get back and report to me here. Any questions?"

"No. I'll come right back."

"Right back!"

He felt good now, thinking back on how it had gone. Olive was on his way—the ace he unfortunately had to play. But that was the game. Thank God he'd had the foresight to have him ready. And then, better still, he had his extra ace. Or, as the thought suddenly occurred to him, his wild deuce.

He took another look at himself in the mirror. It wouldn't be long now. Not long at all.

This time the knock on the door was softer, and he felt the wonderful little tossing in his heart as he strode across the room and opened it.

"Darling, I'm late. I'm terrible sorry."

"You're not late, my dear. Time is where you are," he said, "and so time is here."

"Horatio, you're a poet!"

He closed the door behind her. "I thought we might

enjoy a glass of sherry. I had them bring some early on."

"How delightful. And did your business go well?"

His eyes covered her from head to toe as she crossed the room and sat down. He felt absolutely marvelous. "My business couldn't have have gone better, my dear," he said, handing her a glass of sherry.

"And was that your great idea?"

"Which great idea are you referring to?" he said with a confiding chuckle.

"You've mentioned it a couple of times, but we've always been interrupted one way or another."

He smiled at her, his brows knitting as he searched his memory. At the same time he thought how magnificent her particular beauty was. Such a lady! And in bed, such a delightful animal! And suddenly he remembered.

"Of course, how odd. I keep forgetting it, and when I remember it you're not around. But it is my master stroke, and I'm going to tell it to you, and we're going to drink to it right now." He raised his glass.

"I can't wait to hear what it is. If you don't tell me right this minute I'll burst."

They both laughed at that. "We'll have a sip first," he said, nursing the moment.

"Tell me."

"Well, as a matter of fact I was thinking something very simple, very direct, and in the long run, I believe, very profitable." He took a sip of sherry. "I have decided to change my name."

"Change your name? To what?" She was staring at him in utter surprise. "You don't mean forever. Or is it just a sort of alias for a while?"

"No, I have my name and I like it. Horatio Kyle. It's a good name. And I'm going to keep it."

"Then—"

"I have decided that I need something, and so—how can I put it? I'm going to ennoble myself. That's it! I shall now be known as Lord Kyle."

Her hand flew to her mouth as she stared at him in complete surprise. "But that's a wonderful idea! Why didn't you think of that sooner?"

"I wanted to wait for the right moment."

"But my heavens, Horatio, I can see that your meeting did go well! Very well indeed, My Lord Horatio Kyle." And putting down her drink she rose and came over and threw her arms around him.

Suddenly something occurred to her and she stood back. "But don't you have to be appointed to that, or be English or something?"

"My dear, we are in America, a country where anything can happen, and as long as you don't offend too many people, no one gives a damn."

She beamed at him. "I think we need another meeting, Milord, since the last one appears to have gone so well."

"I fully agree with you, Milady. I think we should address ourselves to that situation—or rather, uh, undress ourselves to that situation." And with their voices tailing off they happily left the room to their echoes and the dying sunlight slanting through the windows.

11

Slocum caught up with them at the old buffalo crossing where they had made camp. It was just getting to be evening, and the sky was soft with the dying light. They were at the edge of a meadow, near the water, and had built a fire just before Slocum got there. Millecent cooked up some stew with the buffalo meat they'd brought with them, and they had corn and canned peaches and good coffee.

"I ain't et that good since I was at one o' them fancy-pants dinin' palaces on Nob Hill in San Francisco," Slocum said, laying on a thick and slightly bawdy western accent, to the delight of his companions.

"And neither have we since . . ." She looked at Frederick. "Gaston à la Bonne Soupe, my dear!"

"Are we still looking for your two towers?" Slocum asked after a moment.

"Well, that's all we have to go by," Lord Frederick said. "But since I think this has to be maybe our last try, how about you deciding, John? I confess, I'm about ready to give up."

"I'd been thinking about those towers that your uncle mentioned as maybe being two buttes. But then it occurred to me that maybe they could be rimrocks. That's why I suggested meeting you up here on the north fork."

"Are rimrocks those big rocks or mountains over there?" Millecent asked.

"I'd say so. And I was thinking of something else. Both of you said Uncle Harry was buried in a shallow grave, and so did the old undertaker I talked to in Drover."

Lord Frederick picked right up on that. "What does that mean, then? Is there something in that?"

"Well, I don't know. Except that it's usually the rule to bury someone pretty deep so the wolves or any other predators can't get at the body."

"So?"

They were both looking at him questioningly.

"So maybe whoever buried him couldn't dig deep."

"Because of the soil?"

"I say 'maybe.' So it wouldn't be around a place like this where the ground is soft. It might likely be higher where digging is tough."

"You mean like up there, over there?" Millecent said, pointing to the high ground she'd mentioned before.

"Maybe. But let's sleep on it. And tomorrow we can take a look-see."

He stood up and began kicking out the fire. "No need for us to heat up the whole country," he said. "Especially since it isn't all that cold."

Later, as he unrolled his bedding, he told himself there was also no sense in heating whoever it was who was following them. But when the girl came later on he said nothing about that.

"I don't know if you want me tonight; I rather think not," she said. "But I did want to let you know that's all right."

"I have to do some scouting," he said. "But there are other nights." And he touched the side of her face.

"Is there danger?"

"I don't think so. Maybe curiosity."

"Is someone following us?"

"That's what I'm going to find out. But they're not going to do anything if they are. I'll be watching. You get some sleep."

"You're a good man, John Slocum."

"Well, you're a good lady."

"No. I don't mean it like that. I mean, you were going to scout to see to our protection, letting me think maybe you didn't want me, but only because you didn't want to frighten me. I call that being a good man."

"Get some sleep," he told her. "Just remember the good thing about lost time is the good time you'll have making up for it."

He didn't scout his back trail, knowing there was one horse and rider, and not wanting to risk letting the man know he was aware of him. But he stayed awake a long time, putting it all together, and then when he slept it was only half sleep, just below the surface.

He was up before dawn. He told Millecent to build a fire and boil coffee, and they had breakfast, the aroma of their coffee mixing with the green, wet morning smells of the land and the fresh smell of their horses as they chomped the lush meadow grass. But they didn't linger; they mounted up just as the sun was touching the horizon.

"We'll cross the river yonder," Slocum said, "and see

if we can find a trail going up by those big humps."

The day broke swiftly, and with all the silence and sounds of the animals, the birds, and the air itself that told of the beginning of a new day. It didn't take them long to find the trail on the other side of the river. It was an old game trail, seldom used, Slocum told them, but it led straight up the side of the steep rise of ground.

It was hot now as they rode along the trail, moving upward slowly toward the high crown above. It was cooler once they got into the spruce and pine. Slocum kept checking their back trail, but there was no sign of the man following them. Yet he knew he was still there.

Twice they stopped to rest the horses and themselves, and the sun was straight up in the sky when they came to an opening out of the trees that gave onto a wider trail.

There was a spring here, and they dismounted and drank and let their horses drink too.

"It's like wine, this water," Lord Frederick said.

They were high up, but Slocum knew they couldn't be seen from below. Nor could they see the valley they had come up from.

Now he told them to lead their horses as he started along the trail, which was not now so steep as it had been. In a few minutes they were in the trees again, with the trail narrower, so they had to go single file. Slocum was looking for sign all along the way, but he saw nothing other than animal signs—deer and coyote.

Then suddenly they broke into a clearing and found themselves on a high, grass-covered ledge that overlooked the great valley below, sweeping down to the river and on up the other side.

"My God," whispered Lord Frederick, breathing the words more than actually speaking them.

Millecent simply drew in her breath and let it out.

"Maybe this is Uncle Harry's gold mine," Slocum said. "It sure has got gold all over it."

And indeed it had. The golden light was everywhere —on the treetops, the rocks, on each blade of grass, on their horses, and on themselves. It washed over the whole of the land, penetrating down into the earth, and they felt it in their skin, coming through into their bodies.

"My God, what a country." Lord Frederick had seated himself on a rock and had drawn up his knees and was simply gazing out.

They were silent for a long time; and then Slocum left them. There was still the fact of the man following them. And it would not do to let his guard down. He crossed the open area and looked at a place where long ago there had been a campfire. There were some rocks left from the campsite. Whoever it was had not tried to hide. Close by, in the lee of a rock he found some empty cartridge shells. Whoever had been there had packed a Henry rifle. He wondered what he'd been shooting at.

When the Edgertons joined him he was looking at a stone that was partly buried at the root of a large pine tree and must have been there some while, for part of it was overgrown with roots, and a lot of pine needles had filled in around the base of the tree as well.

Just beyond the stand of pine was a huge pile of rocks that was evidently the result of a landslide.

"What have you found there?" asked Frederick coming up, and all at once he bent down at the base of the pine tree and began scraping away the pine needles and roots.

"What is it?" asked Millecent, who had joined him. "What have you found?" They were staring down at a carving on the piece of flat rock that Frederick had dug out.

"You know what that figure is?" Slocum said.

"It's my family coat of arms, or at least part of it," Frederick said in a shaky voice.

Millecent started to say something, but Slocum touched her. "Don't turn around, don't speak. Act naturally."

He had seen nothing, but there had been that small stone that someone or maybe a horse had dislodged. It had come just as Millecent had started to speak.

Slocum was already moving away from them. "I'm going over yonder by that pile of rocks. You both stay here, and don't let anyone who might come see that rock. Then follow after me after you count ten."

He was gone. Once behind the rocks he began to circle back to a fresh position. He was still carrying his Winchester, which on dismounting he had pulled from its scabbard. The stone that had rolled had come from down the trail, so there was no immediate danger, but the man could be closer in minutes, especially seeing that he had given himself away.

He watched the pair coming after him now, first heading around the landslide. "Stay over there," he said in a soft voice, and he saw them stop. He figured they were all out of view of the tracker. Although he realized there could be another one coming up behind the first man.

He moved now to a new position so that he had a view of the trail coming out of the stand of trees, which they had taken about twenty minutes ago. But if the tracker was smart, he would find another way to come, having given himself away.

Slocum moved back down to the Edgertons, behind

the rock landslide. "You stay here. Keep your guns ready. Don't shoot unless somebody tries to shoot you. And don't stay so close together."

"Where will you be?"

"I'll see who our visitor is." And he left them. He was mighty glad to see how well they were taking it.

He had just moved into a cluster of spruce when he saw him.

"Slocum!"

Olive was afoot, and he came slowly out of the trail that opened into the clearing.

"Slocum, I know you're here. Come on out. I'm alone, and I'm calling you, you sonofabitch!"

He had walked with slow steps toward the pile of rock landslide, and now he stopped. "Slocum!" He spat angrily at the hard ground. "I know you're here with them two. Come on out and face me like a man, you yellow liver!"

Slocum had been slowly making his way around to where he could see Olive from the side. There was something too pat about the way Olive had arrived. Why had he waited? Why hadn't he called him before. It was when Slocum moved again that he saw the second man. He was behind a rock, with his rifle covering the area where Olive was standing just a few feet below.

Quickly and quietly Slocum pulled off his boots and slipped closer to the man, and then he saw it was Elihu. Elihu had his back to him, his eyes intent on the spot below, where Slocum would appear to confront Olive. Neat, but it had hair on it. Olive should have thought up something better than that. It took only a minute to slip up directly behind Elihu, while Olive was still calling out Slocum's name.

Slocum laid the barrel of his Colt neatly along the

back of Elihu's neck, numbing him instantly.

He had pigging string with him, and he hog-tied and gagged Elihu while he lay inert. Then he crept back to the stand of spruce and called out to Olive that he was coming down.

"Elihu is out of the picture, Olive. You'll have to do your own shooting," he said as he stepped into view.

He saw the surprise sweep into Olive's face as Slocum walked slowly toward him. It was too much for Olive. As Slocum got within a few feet of him Olive held out his hands. "I ain't gonna draw on you, Slocum," he said. "Let's forget it."

"You called me, Olive. Now draw!"

Slocum had stopped walking now and stood absolutely still, ready to draw on the man who had challenged him. Yet he realized that something was wrong. Olive wasn't the kind to challenge a man and then back down. He'd set him up for a drygulching, though. Or had he? And then it hit him. Kyle or somebody had set it up for Olive to get it. Because Olive wanted to beat him in a gunfight, but somebody else—it had to be Kyle—wasn't sure he could win it. Or had Kyle figured to get rid of Olive as well? He knew it was what Olive was thinking. Yes, it figured.

"Slocum, I'm throwing down my guns." And carefully, with his right hand still raised, Olive unbuckled with his left hand and his guns dropped to the ground.

"Some sonofabitch double-crossed me," he said. And he stepped forward away from his two guns lying on the ground.

Slocum watched the struggle in the man's face as he stopped now and stood facing him.

"Get on and get out, then," Slocum said. "And don't let me see you again."

Olive gave a brief nod and turned to go, except that he didn't turn. Instead he dropped to one knee, his right hand streaking to the hideout in his shirt, and then it was out in his big hand. But he never used it.

Slocum's bullet took him right between the eyes. And Olive fell face-down, lying with his dead head right between his two unused Colt .44s. He was still gripping his unfired Smith & Wesson.

From somewhere a horse nickered.

"Real fast there, my friend," said a familiar voice. And looking across to where the trail entered, Slocum saw Stonebraker walking in.

"Thought you'd never get here, you old buzzard," Slocum said, reloading and then dropping his gun into its holster.

"Glad you didn't take it serious, me heading down to Cheyenne."

"I know you better than that. Not with all this action up here, you wouldn't."

He turned to face Lord Frederick and Lady Millecent as they came out from behind the rocks.

"So what's all that?" Stonebraker asked, looking sour at the avalanche.

"That's the Lost and Found Coker Mine," Slocum said. And he added, "Somewhere I reckon. But maybe still lost in that pile of stone. You want to start moving it?"

"I sent a telegram to the marshal's office in Cheyenne to pick up Kyle."

"I got Elihu Burlingame up yonder in piggin' string. He'll have two heads on him by now when he should be coming round."

Millecent came close to where they were standing

and suddenly looked down at Olive. Then she fainted into her husband's arms.

"Kyle has beat it," Stonebraker said, walking into the Doggone Eatery and confronting Slocum and his morning coffee.

"You surprised?"

"Can't say I am."

"How about his lady friend? I heard she was a looker."

"Gone too, but not empty-handed, by God."

"What did they get away with?"

"Plenty. And there is a few sad-looking gentlemen of high finance wondering what hit them."

"But Kyle lost the Coker anyway," Slocum said. "Course, it might be a dud in the end. I mean, if they ever get that landslide dug out."

"Didn't you see how quiet it was here this morning?" Stonebraker said, reaching for the coffee the waitress brought. "They're all out hustling to get to the Coker. Won't do 'em any good. It happens to be on Injun land. The Army's gonna handle it."

"That might be hard on the Edgertons," Slocum said.

"I reckon they can pig it through," Stonebraker replied, sour as a lemon. "Though I can't say they weren't a nice young couple."

"Elihu still locked up?"

Stonebraker nodded. "I'll be takin' him back with me. The rest of 'em have flown, exceptin' the woman who was posin' as the reverend's missus. I don't know what charge we could tack on her."

"I don't think she did much of anything," Slocum said. And Stonebraker cut his eye fast at him, and he felt it. "She's got the kid to look after," he said. "And hell, maybe she can learn how to teach school if maybe she doesn't know already."

"I'll be a sonofabitch," Stonebraker said, jamming an old cigar butt into his teeth.

"What's the matter? You won it, didn't you? You busted up the game."

"Thing is, I went to the wagon out there to question that woman an' she'd flown the nest. Left the kid with a family, I found out."

"Well, you know she probably isn't with Kyle, since he's already got a woman. And she sure ain't with Elihu."

"If you run into her, let me know," the lawman said, his voice friendly as vinegar.

"I sure will," Slocum said, getting to his feet.

"Well, at least you didn't interfere too much," Stonebraker said, striking a match on his thumbnail. "Slocum, watch your back trail."

"Well, at least I'll always know where I can find you, Mr. Stonebraker." And with a nod that wasn't all that friendly he dropped his money on the counter and walked out.

The room clerk wasn't at the desk when he entered the hotel, and when he got upstairs and into his room, Charlie was sitting there.

"You hear about Elihu?" he asked.

She nodded. "Elihu can take care of himself."

Slocum stood there looking at her. She did seem a whole lot different. Like she'd been through it. "I reckon you'll have to take care of yourself too, my friend."

"I thought you were interested."

"I guess I was. But I'm not now. Sorry, Charlie."

She stood up, a sort of smile at her lips, but she kept

her eyes down. He didn't think she was crying. "Well, that's the way the wind blows. Walk me downstairs for a cup of coffee?"

"I could stand a cup."

"You know, I never could make good coffee myself. Elihu was always hollering at me about it."

He had just closed the door of his room behind him when it hit him. The girl was about three feet ahead of him, and he caught the shadow thrown by the sunlight coming through the window at the top of the stairs. In the simultaneity of that instant he had drawn and fired. He felt the bullet hit the wall by his head, and he heard Charlie's muffled scream as the man who had tried to kill him tumbled down the stairs, shot through the lungs.

As Slocum knelt down beside him, Stonebraker's eyes opened.

"How did you figger it, Slocum?" His lips were barely moving, but Slocum heard.

"First, the funny way Olive was when he called me. I figure he was thrown when I told him about Elihu— probably didn't know whether Elihu was there to back him or back-shoot him. Then the girl: there was only one way she could have known about Elihu." He waited a moment. "Why did you do it, old-timer? Kyle, huh."

"He was afraid you knew too much . . . and when Olive and Elihu fucked up I saw I had to . . . Hell, I guess I got too old for this goddamn regulating . . ." He stopped, struggling to breathe. His lips moved. Slocum just barely heard him. "Told you to watch yer back trail, Slocum . . ."

Down the corridor leading to the dining room a door slammed. And Stonebraker was dead.

When he entered the Stud the first person he saw was The Allen.

"Slocum, I am gonna whip your goddamn—"

The hadn't finished the sentence before Slocum doubled him with a driving left into the pit of the stomach, and then followed instantly with the same chopping right hook he'd used twice before on the giant.

The fell poleaxed to the floor of his own saloon. For the third time in a row Slocum had knocked him cold.

The bed surely needed oiling, for the springs were screeching and wailing under their pounding passion. For a moment Slocum even thought the whole thing would collapse.

He had entered her gently, taking time even though his desire was almost more than he could stand. But of all the women he had encountered in Little Misery— and in some other places, too—it was Nellie he favored most. Nellie O'Leary, the madam, was a real lady, a person. And as he told her when the bed finally did collapse—though without interrupting them by even a breath—she was a wonderful lay as well.

"You know something, Slocum," she said as they rested, entwined in each other's arms and legs, "I'd sure rather be a good lay than a good lady."

"And I rather you would too," Slocum said as he rolled over on top of her and her legs opened and she drew up her knees, as her thighs and buttocks and pelvis and all the rest began to meet his rhythm.

JAKE LOGAN

___ 0-425-09088-4	THE BLACKMAIL EXPRESS	$2.50
___ 0-425-09111-2	SLOCUM AND THE SILVER RANCH FIGHT	$2.50
___ 0-425-09299-2	SLOCUM AND THE LONG WAGON TRAIN	$2.50
___ 0-425-09567-3	SLOCUM AND THE ARIZONA COWBOYS	$2.75
___ 0-425-09647-5	SIXGUN CEMETERY	$2.75
___ 0-425-09783-8	SLOCUM AND THE WILD STALLION CHASE	$2.75
___ 0-425-10116-9	SLOCUM AND THE LAREDO SHOWDOWN	$2.75
___ 0-425-10419-2	SLOCUM AND THE CHEROKEE MANHUNT	$2.75
___ 0-425-10347-1	SIXGUNS AT SILVERADO	$2.75
___ 0-425-10555-5	SLOCUM AND THE BLOOD RAGE	$2.75
___ 0-425-10635-7	SLOCUM AND THE CRACKER CREEK KILLERS	$2.75
___ 0-425-10701-9	SLOCUM AND THE RED RIVER RENEGADES	$2.75
___ 0-425-10758-2	SLOCUM AND THE GUNFIGHTER'S GREED	$2.75
___ 0-425-10850-3	SIXGUN LAW	$2.75
___ 0-425-10889-9	SLOCUM AND THE ARIZONA KIDNAPPERS	$2.95
___ 0-425-10935-6	SLOCUM AND THE HANGING TREE	$2.95
___ 0-425-10984-4	SLOCUM AND THE ABILENE SWINDLE	$2.95
___ 0-425-11233-0	BLOOD AT THE CROSSING	$2.95
___ 0-425-11056-7	SLOCUM AND THE BUFFALO HUNTERS	$2.95
___ 0-425-11194-6	SLOCUM AND THE PREACHER'S DAUGHTER	$2.95
___ 0-425-11265-9	SLOCUM AND THE GUNFIGHTER'S RETURN	$2.95
___ 0-425-11314-0	THE RAWHIDE BREED	$2.95

Please send the titles I've checked above. Mail orders to:

BERKLEY PUBLISHING GROUP
390 Murray Hill Pkwy., Dept. B
East Rutherford, NJ 07073

NAME _____

ADDRESS _____

CITY _____

STATE _____ ZIP _____

Please allow 6 weeks for delivery.
Prices are subject to change without notice.

POSTAGE & HANDLING:
$1.00 for one book, $.25 for each
additional. Do not exceed $3.50.

BOOK TOTAL	$_____
SHIPPING & HANDLING	$_____
APPLICABLE SALES TAX (CA, NJ, NY, PA)	$_____
TOTAL AMOUNT DUE PAYABLE IN US FUNDS. (No cash orders accepted.)	$_____